"All that is the past— the dead, forgotten past."

Ginny's eyes were bright with tears as she continued, "What happened then can't happen now. It can't ever be now."

"*This* is now," Ry snapped. "You and me, here."

"You haven't changed, Ry. You're still the same irresponsible drifter. But *I've* changed! Sneer at the new, practical me if you want. But it *is* me, and I'm no longer the impressionable sixteen-year-old you once knew!"

She went on shakily, "And you can't talk me out of marrying Miles. I love him, even if he *is* rich!"

Ry looked into Ginny's face, as though to check that she'd stopped crying, then kissed her mouth with warm tenderness. "I'll come for you one of these fine days, Ginny. Count on it."

MADELEINE KER is a self-described "compulsive writer." In fact, Madeleine has been known to deliver six romances in less than a year. She is married and lives in Spain.

Books by Madeleine Ker

HARLEQUIN ROMANCE

2595—VOYAGE OF THE MISTRAL
2636—THE STREET OF THE FOUNTAIN
2709—ICE PRINCESS
2716—HOSTAGE

HARLEQUIN PRESENTS

642—AQUAMARINE
656—VIRTUOUS LADY
672—PACIFIC APHRODITE
699—THE WINGED LION
739—WORKING RELATIONSHIP
778—OUT OF THIS DARKNESS
795—FIRE OF THE GODS
884—DANGER ZONE
947—IMPACT
1090—FRAZER'S LAW
1114—THE WILDER SHORES OF LOVE
1138—JUDGEMENT
1185—STORMY ATTRACTION

TROUBLEMAKER

Madeleine Ker

Harlequin Books

TORONTO • NEW YORK • LONDON
AMSTERDAM • PARIS • SYDNEY • HAMBURG
STOCKHOLM • ATHENS • TOKYO • MILAN

Original hardcover edition published in 1988
by Mills & Boon Limited

ISBN 0-373-03017-7

Harlequin Romance first edition November 1989

Printed in U.S.A.

CHAPTER ONE

'THANK YOU, Mr Edwards. Good morning.'

Ginny stamped the paying-in book, passed it back to the customer, and wrapped a last rubber band round the untidy stack of money. Larry Edwards, the village butcher, always banked his morning's takings at this time of day. It was not just her fancy that the money often smelt of blood. There were sometimes a few crumbs of mincemeat clinging to the notes too.

Money was money. She glanced out through the plate-glass window as she put the notes into her till. It was coming up for lunch time, and there was only one customer left in the queue.

He was male, very tall, and made anonymous in a slightly sinister way by the black motorcyle leathers and full-face helmet he wore. The sort of ominous character who turns out to be the sadistic bank robber in films, but who in real life was invariably a messenger, whose only crime had been to park his bike on the double yellow lines outside the bank.

She gave the smoked glass visor of the helmet a smile. 'Yes?'

Silently, he passed an envelope over the counter to her with a black-gloved hand. Her full name, GINA NORTHCLIFFE, was written on it.

Ginny opened it. What it contained was not a message. Or at least, not the kind of message that official messengers delivered. It wasn't money or an account credit, either. It wasn't anything to do with bank business at all.

It was a crudely printed note, which read:

HAND OVER ALL THE MONEY NOW OR I WILL BLOW THIS BANK UP

Ginny's heart froze in a moment of sheer horror. It was her nightmare come true. A real, broad-daylight robbery in Grantley!

Unable to move, she could only stare wide-eyed at the smooth white dome of the helmet, and the impenetrable black visor which hid the criminal's face.

She was so frightened that not a word of the correct drill came in her mind. Was she supposed to hand the money over, press the alarm buzzer under the counter, neither, or both?

Then the black gloves lifted slowly to the helmet, and eased it off, and Ginny found herself staring into a pair of laughing eyes that were the deepest blue she had ever seen, so deep that they were only a shade off violet.

'I'm dynamite,' said the 'bank robber' in a deep voice. 'Hi, cutie. Feel like lighting my fuse?'

Ginny sagged in her seat, and raised shaky hands to her face.

'My God. You utter *pig!*'

'Aren't you pleased to see me?'

'I nearly pressed the panic button,' she croaked. 'And it would have served you right, Ryan Savage!' She picked up the note. 'I ought to show this to Miles, right now!'

'Now, now.' The brilliant eyes were totally unabashed. 'Where do your loyalties lie?'

'To the bank, of course!'

'Of course,' he repeated with wicked meaning. 'To the bank—and its revered manager, Miles Langton.' He leaned on the counter, muscular shoulders tightening through the black leather. The face was the same, just a little older. The same rugged nose and cheekbones, the same cleft in the aggressive chin, the same half-smile on the wide mouth that looked as though it had kissed a thousand women.

Even his hair, thick and black as night, and worn far too long, was the same. It curled over his ears, reaching almost to the shoulders of the leather jacket, but not quite obscuring the glint of a golden earring in one ear.

And the same unforgettable eyes, clear and wicked as blue diamonds.

'You swore you'd wait for me,' he went on accusingly. 'Couldn't you hang on for eighteen months?'

'Eighteen months is a long time.' She heard the defensiveness in her voice.

'Anyway, you don't look a day older.' His eyes appraised her breasts with complete male approval, about the only part of her figure he could see from where he stood. 'In fact, you look ravishing, Ginny darling. Just gorgeous.' He grinned. 'I've come to claim you. Hop over the counter, and let's elope to the Fiji Islands.'

Ginny tried to summon her scattered wits. 'You haven't changed much either, and that is *not* a compliment. I'm going to have nightmares about this.' She glanced over her shoulder to see if Miles or any of the others had noticed the exchange, but Ry had picked his moment well. No one was even looking their way. She turned back to Ryan Savage and showed him her still-trembling hands accusingly. 'Look!'

'Ah! You always were a sucker for my overpowering male appeal.' The eyes, deep and warm as a summer sky, studied her left hand. 'You're looking kind of naked around the third finger, Ginny darling. Don't tell me old Miles is too mean to buy you a ring?'

'Sssh!' she hushed him, knowing how easily voices—especially voices as deep and strong as Ry's—could carry in the hushed atmosphere of the bank. 'I don't wear it to work.'

'Why not?' Ry wanted to know, drumming his gloved fingers on his helmet and watching her.

'Just security.'

Ry made a snorting sound. 'Security. Does he make you

sleep with your hand in a safe at night? Listen, how are you? You can tell me over lunch. I've booked a table at the Cuban Hat. Is the chilli still as hot as ever?'

Ginny couldn't suppress a smile, weak as she still was. The Cuban Hat had always been Ry's favourite eating-place, a haunt of bikers and truckers, and Grantley's only claim to a low-life dive. 'I haven't been to the Cuban Hat in years,' she informed him, 'and I'm certainly not going today, with *you* of all people.'

'With *me* of all people?' he repeated in mock-astonishment. 'What am I, contagious?'

'You're a troublemaker,' she said primly, pursing her neat mouth. 'I always have lunch with Miles, anyway. At the Willows.'

'The Willows!' Ry blew a whistle of ironic awe. 'Can you stand the pace?'

'Miles's taste in restaurants, as in everything else,' she replied primly, 'is impeccable. The cuisine at the Willows is very good, as it happens.'

'Cui-sine?' He looked even more impressed. 'That's a fancy word for overcooked food, isn't it?' One eyebrow lifted, an old, old mannerism. 'You must be the only female in the place without the obligatory blue rinse, nylon teeth and twin set.'

Ginny tried not to giggle. She checked once more that none of her colleagues were watching, then rested her chin in her hands, and gazed at him with big brown eyes. 'This is the best way to see you,' she reflected. 'Through plate glass, with the police only a button-push away. How are you, Ry?'

'Fighting fit.' And indeed, he looked extraordinarily well. But for the leathers, the long hair—oh, and the quarter-inch stubble that covered his jaw and upper lip—he would easily have been the handsomest man she had ever seen. Who was she kidding? He *was* the handsomest man she'd ever seen. Her expression was dreamy as the memories came flooding back.

Especially one memory, now nearly six years old, but

fresh as this morning's paint. A memory of a heart-stopping joyride in a 'borrowed' sports car, and of a vivid half-hour parked at the edge of a wheatfield . . .

'You do realise that if you won't come to lunch with me, I really *will* blow this joint up?' Ry glanced behind her, then raised his voice a notch. 'Does Brother Miles know about that night in the Maserati? The unexpurgated version? I'll bet you and he have some good chuckles over that.'

'Ry!' she muttered, hunching as though ducking a low-flying bullet. She peered over her shoulder. Miles was emerging from his doorway carrying a sheaf of papers. He looked her way, the light glancing off his spectacles, but didn't seem to notice anything amiss, for he stooped busily over Vera Davidson's desk with some query.

Ginny was relieved. Miles knew perfectly well that she and Ryan Savage had once been—well, what had they been? Teenage sweethearts? Anyhow, Miles knew quite enough about Ry to be upset by Ry's resurfacing like this. The last thing she wanted was to upset him.

'Good God.' Ry was squinting with a comical expression at Miles's back. 'What some girls will do for security! Where did he get that cheap toupee?'

'It's not a toupee,' she snapped. Miles had changed his hairstyle shortly after they'd got engaged, to a style she suspected he thought 'younger'. Not everyone had liked the change, but she hadn't had the heart to tell him it didn't suit him. Nor had she enjoyed that crack about what some girls would do for security. It wasn't the first time she'd had *that* thrown at her. 'Keep your voice down. And don't make disgusting assumptions!'

Ry had never been the sort of man who reacted to orders from anyone. 'You mean you're not marrying him for the money?' he asked in the same carrying tone.

'Ry, *hush*!'

'I mean it.' He rasped a thumb up his chin, eyes laughing at her. 'You'd better get out of that lunch date at the morgue, or I'm going to do something truly embarrassing.'

'I *can't.*' She buried herself in her till, still offended. 'And if you haven't got any bank business, you can't just stand there!'

'Who says?' He pulled off one black glove, revealing a strong, lean hand that was as tanned as the rest of him, and extracted a cheque book from inside his jacket. 'Give me a pen.'

'*You* with a cheque book?' She gave him some of his own eyebrow-raising medicine, but passed him the pen all the same. 'What are you doing back here, anyway?'

'I've come to see the leafy lanes of my childhood. And to look up a few old friends. Like you.'

She stuck her tongue out at him, and he sighed.

'This isn't much of a homecoming,' he said, scribbling out the cheque with decisive strokes. 'Why is no one in my beloved home town pleased to see me back?'

'I told you—you're a troublemaker. Nobody wants to see you.'

He glanced up at her briefly, and something in his eyes wiped the smile off her lips. A pang of guilt stung her heart. Ry had feelings too. Maybe it *did* hurt to be rejected quite as regularly as he was in a stuffy little place like Grantley.

There had been a time when she'd have been overwhelmed with joy to see him back. But not now, not any more.

'Cash that for me,' he commanded, passing the cheque across, and flipping a card on to it.

'Your trouble,' she said, more gently, 'was being born in a quiet little English town like this one. You'd have been in your element somewhere like Brooklyn, or downtown Chicago.' She glanced at the cheque, and did a double-take. 'Five hundred pounds?'

'I need the money to show you a good time,' he said, dropping her a slow wink.

Ginny's mouth was so full that it was usually almost an oval, but caution now compressed it into a narrow pink leaf. 'I'll have to get confirmation on this.'

Those extraordinary eyes were made all the more beautiful by thick, long eyelashes that would have been the envy of any starlet. When he drooped them languidly, the effect could either be devastatingly sexy, or—as in this case—stingingly contemptuous. 'Confirm away,' he drawled.

It was on the tip of her tongue to ask whether this was another joke, but she bit the suggestion back. With a nod to him, she slipped off her stool and took the cheque to Rita on Enquiries, for referral back to the London branch where the account was kept.

'Thought so,' Rita said with muffled excitement, peering at the cheque through her thick glasses. 'I knew it was Ry Savage as soon as he walked in through the door!' They both glanced across to where Ry was lounging against the counter, with his inimitable air of owning the place. The black leathers hugged his figure, emphasising the broad shoulders, lithe waist and long, muscular legs of the perfect male body. 'Ooh,' Rita sighed, 'he's *gorgeous!* All *man.* He hasn't been back in years.'

'Double-check everything,' Ginny advised her drily, tapping the cheque with an oval fingernail. 'We don't want any mistakes.'

The slight emphasis on *mistakes* made the girl's eyes widen behind the milk-bottle lenses. 'You don't think he's trying to——?'

'No, I don't. But double-check, all the same.'

'Right.' Plump Rita scooped up the telephone, and Ginny turned to face Miles, on his way back into the little reproduction-oak cubicle which—it was a small branch—went under the name of 'The Manager's Office'.

'Ginny!' He crooked a finger to summon her. She obeyed, with an odd squirmy feeling that he'd recognised Ry, and was about to demand an explanation for his presence here.

But once inside his office, he smiled at her apologetically. 'Brewster MacElvoy wants me to join him for lunch. Sorry.'

Ginny stared for a moment in surprise. That left her free to take up Ryan Savage's invitation after all. If she wanted to.

'He's a pest,' Miles went on, taking her reaction for disappointment, 'but an important pest.' He tugged his moustache. 'Much as I'd like to put him off for your sake . . .'

'No, of course not,' she said. Clients were always inviting Miles to lunch at short notice, and Brewster, a local farmer, was one of the biggest account-holders in Grantley. A substantial loan to buy extra land had been in the offing for a few weeks, and Brewster probably wanted to discuss that over his usual lunchtime cottage pie and half-pint. Half-pint of whisky, that was. 'Just don't let him get you too drunk,' she smiled.

'I won't. Shall I cancel the Willows? Or do you want to go ahead on your own?'

She glanced over her shoulder, then reversed the movement guiltily, but Miles didn't pick it up. Should she tell him about Ry, after all? No. Firstly because Miles was very sensitive about younger men hovering around her, and secondly because Ry was not the sort of man Miles would have been tolerant about, even if he'd been sixty. She curled a lock of chestnut hair round her finger. 'Er—no. No, I'll just have a snack at the—er—burger bar.' Funny how easily that lie had slipped out!

'Sure?'

'Sure.'

'Sorry,' Miles said again, touching her arm. He looked younger than his forty-six years. Everybody said so. He was always immaculately shaven, apart from the trim moustache which helped to add character to his face, and he had what people called 'dress sense'. In his dapper grey suit and modern, dark-rimmed glasses, he was the very antithesis of Ryan Savage.

Miles meant a lot in Grantley, and Grantley meant a lot to him. The bank had offered him several transfers to much bigger branches over the years, but he had always refused them. He was determined not be sucked Londonwards, away from the small town where he had been born. Miles was on endless committees. He was chairman of the local Rotary Club, secretary of the golf club, treasurer of the Country Club, and had been an alderman of the town for years. He was an authority on local history, and was writing a book about Grantley in his spare time.

There was nothing any other place could have offered him which could ever match the status and respect he had achieved in Grantley.

Miles would no sooner have taken a transfer to London than he would have taken one to the moon.

Nor did he need the money. Miles's father had left him a rich man, and not just by Grantley standards. He drove a small Austin Rover saloon to work every day, but there was also a brand-new Jaguar in the garage at Greenlawns, his huge house outside the town, and a cabin cruiser on the nearby river.

Ginny wasn't just in love with Miles Langton. She was very proud of him, and she had never quite got over the thrill that he had chosen *her,* out of all the girls in Grantley, as his wife. She smiled at him warmly.

'You don't have to apologise, Miles. I should start watching what I eat, anyway. I don't want to look like a porpoise in my wedding dress.'

'You look fine to me.' His eyes drifted down her figure. 'More than fine.'

'Thank you, kind sir. I'd better get back to the till.' Pleased with the compliment, Ginny blew him a kiss and another smile, and went back to Rita.

'He's got the funds,' Rita informed her, passing back the cheque. She removed her glasses, and patted her hair into place. 'Say hello for me,' she pleaded. 'He'll remember me.'

Ginny pulled a face. But she was feeling another little pang of guilt as she headed back to her stool. She hadn't *really* suspected Ry of trying to pull a fast one with that cheque, but the unworthy thought had been there, all the same.

The contrast between Miles and Ryan Savage was even more strikingly obvious as she looked back into those vivid blue eyes again. Ryan, the dangerous black panther, with the electric coat you just ached to reach out and caress . . .

'Well?' he challenged.

'Oh, you can have your five hundred,' she said, and switched to her bank teller voice. 'How would you like the money, sir?'

'I *know* I can have my five hundred,' he said acidly. 'And I'll have it in fifties. You do keep fifties at this dear little old branch?'

'One or two,' she said sweetly, starting to count them.

'I meant—*well,* have you told Brother Miles you're coming to lunch with me today?'

'No.' Ginny double-checked the ten notes. 'But I will come. If you're discreet.'

'Discreet? Cuisine?' He shook his dark head in mockery. 'My, little Ginny Northcliffe, but you are picking up a lot of cute words these days! So what does discretion entail?'

'Picking me up outside the sweetshop at one-fifteen,' she commanded, and passed him the money. 'And not *ever* coming here while I'm at the till!'

'The sweetshop is two streets away.' He smiled lazily. 'Are you really that ashamed of me?'

'Miles knows——' Ginny bit her lip to cut off the foolish cliché. But Ry took up her words with a grin.

'Miles knows about us? My God! What are we going to do, darling?'

She avoided the mocking question. 'Rita Westbrooke is working on Enquiries. She said to say hello.'

She followed Ry's eyes as he looked across at Rita. He raised a gloved hand to his lips, and blew a slow, sultry kiss in her direction. Rita's round face went pink with pleasure, and with a little wave she disappeared round the corner like a rabbit going down a burrow.

Ry grinned back at Ginny, beautiful teeth white as ice against his tanned lips. 'See you at the sweetshop, lollipop.' He slid the money into his jacket, and walked towards the door.

Ginny watched his broad back, her eyes trailing down to take in his sexy bottom and hard, leather-clad haunches, his long legs encased in beautiful motorcycle boots. He turned to give her a last smile over his shoulder, black-haired and blue-eyed, before going out.

She sighed as the door closed behind him. Rebellious male sexuality personified—that was Ryan Savage. And he hadn't changed one little bit.

You swore you'd wait for me! If only she'd thought he would ever settle down to a proper career and a respectable life, like everyone else, she might have done just that, for twenty years if needs be . . .

Some chance. Ry wasn't the settling down kind, even though he must by now be—she did a quick calculation. She herself was twenty-two this year. That made Ry something around twenty-six. And whatever mysterious jobs he did up there in the Big Smoke, which enabled him to draw five-hundred-pound cheques, she'd bet her life they weren't proper or respectable.

A smile crept across her mouth as her mind went back five, ten, fifteen years into the past. There had always been a Ry Savage in her life, a thrilling, dark presence you were forbidden to associate with, to be glimpsed thundering along the quiet lanes in a beat-up motorcycle, or to be encountered leaning against a fence, whistling, with those amazing blue eyes laughing at you.

She'd first grown aware of him as a real person when she'd started high school. By that time, Ry had been in his final year, and she, like every other pigtailed junior, had held him in a mixture of adoration and terror.

Everyone knew he came from a broken home. He lived with his helpless uncle and aunt, who must have sometimes thought of themselves as the keepers of a rapidly developing

Bengal tiger. Where his real parents were, no one knew. His foster-parents weren't the gossipy kind, and Ry never discussed the subject.

That was something which had drawn her to him from the start. Her home had been broken too—not by divorce, but by the early death of her father, an event which had left Ginny with a permanent, deep insecurity.

If Ry felt that same insecurity, though, he reacted to it in a very different way. Indifferent to laws and rules, he was always a troublemaker. He got into fights; he was found drinking in the local pub with poachers and other villains; he was given so many speeding tickets that he was almost jailed; he played practical jokes with alarming consequences.

A wild, violent, unpredictable and destructive force. That was Ryan Savage too. It was Ry who painted the venerable hands of the town clock a tasteful luminous pink. It was Ry who had been caught *in flagrante delicto* with Tina Harpur, the barmaid at the Crown, whom Ginny had always thought of as the most beautiful woman in the world, and who was at least ten years older than Ry.

And it was Ry who had 'borrowed' a Maserati and driven it round the country lanes until the petrol ran out, though very few people knew that Ginny had been in the car with him when the police had finally caught up with them that night.

She and Ry had been going out then. Not lovers, just going out. She'd adored him with every fibre of her teenage heart. And every fibre had snapped with a jolt when he'd left.

The associated parents, police, gamekeepers and schoolmasters of Grantley had heaved a collective sigh of relief when Ry, having somehow managed to get his A-levels, had climbed on to his motorbike and had roared off in the direction of London.

But Ginny had been desolated.

At first she'd missed him with all the passion of a romantic teenager, blaming him furiously for having jilted her like that. He had only been back half a dozen times, the last time at least a year and a half ago. He had always come to see her, always with the same grin and the same command: *swear you'll wait for me!*

She had always been weak-kneed with pleasure at seeing him, even though her schoolgirl crush was starting to fade fast. It was flattering, at any rate, to feel that Ry Savage was still interested in her. She dreamed of his return, all the time.

Until she'd got sick of waiting for Ry. And this time was quite different. A lot of water had passed under the bridge. This time there was Miles to consider. Miles, who knew everything about the little town, also knew that she had once been sweet, *more* than sweet, on Ryan Savage. He'd be very upset by what she was doing now.

In the past eighteen months, moreover, she herself had changed and grown up a great deal, and her once overwhelming feelings for Ry had matured into a much more cool-eyed understanding. As a matter of fact, the arrival of Ry was about as welcome as a fox in a dovecot.

The warm smile faded. It certainly wouldn't do for anyone to see her lunching at the Cuban Hat with Ry. Not within two months of her impending marriage to the most respectable man in Grantley. If word got back to Miles, there would be trouble. Miles would find it hard to understand her motives, and he'd probably suspect the worst. For a man of such importance, he had a very vulnerable ego. He'd be painfully hurt by the thought that his fiancée was still welcoming the attentions of a younger man. And she cared far too much for Miles to let him be hurt.

She prepared to hand over to the lunchtime teller. For Miles' sake, for her own sake, she would have to tread very, very warily.

She waited for him at the sweetshop, a trim figure in a light summer dress. At first sight, careless men sometimes thought Gina Northcliffe unremarkable, with her medium-length chestnut hair and delicate colouring. The nice, ordinary, girl-next-door type.

But there were other things that a second glance revealed, which disproved the judgement. Such as a soft and truly gorgeous mouth, set between a fine nose and a dainty chin. Such as rich brown eyes that were unusually large and unusually lustrous, and filled with intelligent amusement.

When you got around to noticing that her legs were the kind used in advertisements for the finest stockings, and that she moved in exactly the graceful way a young girl was supposed to move, you started realising that Ginny's ordinariness was actually a kind of perfection.

And those of Miles Langton's friends who wondered why he had chosen a woman over twenty years his junior soon stopped wondering, and started envying him instead.

Ginny Northcliffe wasn't beautiful. She was something much better than that. Ginny was desirable. And that was a quality which would stay warm and alive in her long after the surface beauty faded and tarnished.

She had a warm and passionate nature—obstinate, sometimes blindly wilful, but deeply feminine. Even her best friends might have accused her of a certain capacity for self-deception. Combined with that stubborn streak, it sometimes led her into crazy decisions.

Even her *very* best friends might have admitted that Ginny Northcliffe's judgement was not always impeccable.

But of late, there had been rather a dearth of best friends to tell her such things.

Miles had made no secret of the fact that he didn't get on with her circle. In truth, she'd been slightly flattered to be told how much more mature than her friends she was, to be told that she was different from them, special. But it was also painful to watch Miles trying to socialise with the people she'd gone to school with. The gap was so great that he looked almost pathetic, totally unable to join in, or feel at his ease.

Moreover, none of them had really liked Miles. And none of them had approved of the match. Some of the boys, especially those who'd had a crush on her, tended to say deliberately cutting or offensive things to Miles. And of course, that couldn't be tolerated.

The upshot was that she had steadily drifted away from them, and into the much older circle of Miles Langton's friends. Not that she got on particularly well with *them,* but at least Miles was happier with them than with her friends. And they represented her future. Her school friends were firmly in the past.

Come to think of it, it had been weeks since she'd seen any of the old gang.

Going out with Ry this sunny afternoon was going to be her first contact with a man in her own age-bracket for a long, long time!

The deep rumble of the motorcycle preceded Ry's arrival round the corner. The bike was a huge black BMW with silver pinstripes, and its brutal, macho shape suited him to perfection. He pulled up next to her, and jerked his head for her to get on.

'Here we go,' she muttered to herself, her voice lost in the throbbing music of the engine. Tucking her skirt chastely between her thighs, she clambered on to the warm leather seat behind Ry, trying to avoid touching anything greasy with her cream-stockinged calves. He pulled off sharply enough to make her fling her arms round his waist in alarm, and accelerated with a roar down the street.

CHAPTER TWO

SHE tucked her cheek against his shoulder to keep the wind out of her face. The body in her arms was hard, muscular and extremely strong. This was very, very different from cruising in the air-conditioned comfort of Miles's Jaguar. Pray God no one she knew saw her like this, hugging Ry Savage with her arms and thighs while her skirt fluttered up almost to her hips!

The ride to the Cuban Hat was brief, but the contact with Ry had been intimate enough to leave her cheeks still flaming as she slipped off the saddle, and stood back to smooth the creases out of her skirt.

'I should have known better,' she was muttering as he switched the engine off and hauled off his helmet.

'You should have known better than what?' he grinned, locking the bike.

'Thanks for offering me your helmet,' she said acidly, running her short-nailed fingers through her hair. 'I must look like a golliwog.'

'You look like a film star,' he crooned, coming round the machine to her. 'An angel—a dream. Look at you. The wind in your hair, a bit of colour in your cheeks—you look alive at last.'

'Can we get this over with?' Ginny requested, eyeing the somewhat grimy façade of the Cuban Hat bleakly. 'I'm hungry.'

'First,' Ry said, moving purposefully close, 'a proper, hello-nice-to-see-you kiss.'

'No!'

But there was nowhere she could run to. Ry took her in his arms, and bent down to kiss her full on the lips.

Only one man, Miles Langton, had kissed her in

almost two years, and her first overwhelming impression was of warmth.

Miles's kisses were cool, like his skin. Civilised, shaded, indoor kisses that she'd always found quite satisfactory.

But Ry was warm. Warm mouth, big warm body holding hers, and, she registered with shock, a warm tongue gently probing her lips.

Heat flooded her, as though the midsummer sunshine overhead had suddenly been let into her soul through a flung-open window. She fought away from him, squirmed out of his arms, and took two weak steps back.

'Ry, *no*! Don't you *dare* do that again!'

'Ah,' he sighed reminiscently, smiling at her with eyes that were three shades deeper than the sky, 'the leafy lanes of our youth.'

'I'm not sixteen any more.' Ginny laid a hand on her racing heart, as if to steady its mad course, and glared at him. 'Just don't!'

'And you smell heavenly,' he sighed, sniffing at her as though she was a rose. 'You didn't have that perfume on in the bank.'

'I put it on before I came to meet you. At least,' she stumbled over the words, 'b—before I left the bank. It's not for *your* benefit, anyway!'

His laughter was soft, deep as the note of the motorbike. 'Come on, let's eat.'

He led her into the restaurant with a hand firmly grasping her arm.

Restaurant, of course, was a polite word. The Cuban Hat, which cultivated a Mexican-Latin image and cuisine, was set on the turn-off road from the motorway to London, and that made it a popular stopping-off point with truckers and bikers and other professional travellers. It was rough, the car park always filled with lorries and hideously chopped motorbikes, but the food was excellent, and the spicy aromas that hailed them as they walked in through the door were decidedly mouthwatering.

The usual motley crowd of scruffy-to-downright-mean diners were eating with noisy enthusiasm, and Ry found them the quietest possible seat, overlooking the gardens at the back.

With that odd-gallantry that he'd always shown, he ushered Ginny into her chair, made her comfortable, then sat opposite her. And ruined the whole effect by unzipping the leather jacket to his waist, revealing a snowy designer T-shirt that showed practically half his chest.

It was a very tanned, very muscular chest, the broad pectoral muscles etched with crisp black hair. The stomach below it looked as hard as marble under the cotton T-shirt, which seemed to hug every ripple of muscle.

'You're staring,' he purred, tugging off his gloves and dropping them into his upturned helmet. 'Do I shock and offend you?'

'You can only be shocked and offended when you're expecting something better,' she said snippishly. 'I *always* expect the worst from you.'

'How sad.' He flicked the menu over to her. 'You're the expert on cuisine. Pick something sophisticated.'

'Chilli and beans,' she read with distaste. 'Chilli con carne. Tacos. Red-hot tamales and chips. I'm going to smell like Pancho Villa when I get back to the bank.'

'What does *cher* Miles like you to smell of?' Ry asked scornfully. 'Boiled hake and instant mashed potatoes?'

'Miles takes me to places that aren't filled with Hell's Angels and truck-drivers,' she rejoined serenely. 'He treats me like a lady.'

'Stick with me, and you'll see the underside of life,' Ry promised with a glint. 'It's got more pizzazz than the topside, I guarantee.' He snapped brown fingers for the waitress, who suddenly seemed not to be terribly busy after all. 'Tacos and Mexican salad for two,' he commanded, 'and two ice-cold beers.'

Giving him a big smile, the girl headed off with the order, and Ry leaned on the table, pushing his devastatingly handsome face within a foot of Ginny's.

'Now,' he said with mock-aggression, 'explain!'

'Explain what?' she asked, avoiding his eyes.

'This aberration with Miles Langton.' He pointed an accusing finger at her, and for a moment his eyes were truly formidable. 'You promised you'd wait for me, Ginny.'

She gave him a weak smile. 'That old chestnut? I got tired of waiting. You can't just arrive out of nowhere and demand an explanation for the past one and a half years, Ry.'

The thick, well-shaped eyebrows climbed. 'All that time? Has it been going on for that long?'

'That's how long I've been at the bank,' she said, as though that answered the question.

'And in that time, you've decided that you want to spend the rest of your life as Mrs Middle-Class Grantley?'

'You don't know Miles,' she said shortly, 'or you wouldn't be so contemptuous of him.'

'Who says I'm contemptuous of *him*?' Ry asked with a subtle emphasis that made her cheeks flush angrily.

'Contemptuous of me, then. Miles is an extraordinary man. I love him. He's cultured, intelligent and charming.'

'He's also boring, middle-aged and rich.' The sunlight through the window was illuminating Ry's face, turning his skin to gold and his eyes into sapphires—the million-dollar kind. 'How old is he? Fifty? By the time you're my age, Miles will be about ready for a peaceful retirement, with golf every other day and a snooze in the afternoons. Is your *love* going to survive that?' He rasped his thumb against his beard again, a deliberately nerve-setting gesture, and stared into her eyes. 'You're going to be bored out of your clever little skull, darling.'

'Miles is forty-six,' she said coldly. 'By the time I'm

your age, he'll be just over fifty. And he'll still be what he is now—a highly successful and respected man in this community.'

'Success and respect,' he repeated. 'Are those the qualities you're marrying him for?'

'They're not qualities which you admire, I know,' she said nastily. 'But they matter to *me.*'

'I don't give a damn about the kind of success you mean—an overstuffed bank account and a pot belly. As for respect . . .' that lazy smile spread across his mouth, 'I can always get that whenever I want.'

'With your fists?'

'Any way I choose. I'm a genius in my field.' He took her left hand in his, and studied the engagement ring. 'Some bauble. I take it this *is* for my benefit?'

'It's a one-carat blue-white,' she said proudly. She'd put the ring on before leaving the bank. She looked down. Her slim fingers looked fragile in Ry's bronze machine-tools of hands. 'That's a very good stone. It cost a lot of money.'

'No doubt about it.' He stroked the soft skin of her palm with unbelievable gentleness, and smiled at her with eyes that made the diamond look dull. 'What a mercenary little bitch you've turned into,' he said softly.

She jerked her hand away, anger flaring in her. 'Damn you, Ry! You're the bloody limit! Who the hell are you to judge me and what I do?'

'I'm the first man who ever kissed that gorgeous little mouth,' he reminded her with a wicked expression.

'That was a long, long time ago.' She was still angry enough to walk out on him—if she'd had a way of getting back to the town from this dump. 'Not that it's any of your business, but I happen to be very close to Miles. He's been exceptionally kind to Mum and me. Sometimes I think we wouldn't have got by without him.'

'My heart goes out to him. So you're marrying him out of gratitude?'

'I'm marrying him because I care for him!'

The tacos had arrived, and the waitress unloaded the huge platefuls of fragrant food on to their table.

It had been ages since Ginny had eaten anything like this. The tacos were crisp and golden shells, tasting of corn. She loaded mincemeat on to one, and crunched gingerly into it. It was searingly hot, in both senses.

'My God!' she gasped, as soon as she could speak, and reached for the beer. It went down like nectar after the spicy chilli, and she fanned her lips with her napkin. 'You need an asbestos mouth for this stuff!'

'That's why the beer has to be iced.' Ry was eating with practised neatness. 'It's better than boiled hake and mash. Get it down.'

Smiling, she obeyed. The food *was* delicious, despite being so fiery, and when Ry ordered another beer apiece, she didn't object.

'What about you?' she asked, putting the dewy glass down. 'Where are you working?'

'At the moment, over in Newton,' he said, naming one of the nearby villages. 'I like to spend a few weeks of the summer in the countryside.'

'At Lacon's farm, like before?' she asked. He nodded, and Ginny sighed. 'I might have guessed that's why you're so tanned. Oh, Ry, is that what I was supposed to wait for? You make me sad.'

He looked at her quizzically. 'Why?'

'You've got so much potential. When are you going to start some kind of career? You can't spend the rest of your life as a casual labourer on other people's farms.'

'Why not?' he asked.

'Because you could do so much *more*!'

'You mean, be stuck in a bank all day, like you? End up chairman of the Country Club, like Miles Langton?'

'Don't knock it,' she replied. 'You're no spring chicken yourself, you know. You'll have to settle down some time or other.' Her brown eyes narrowed in suspicion. 'How come you're so flash with your money, if you're only doing casual harvesting on farms?'

'I like that *only*,' he grinned. 'It's people like me who put the Weetabix on your breakfast table, darling.'

'And that bike looks new—and pricy.'

'Not to mention the duds.' He tugged the lapel of his admittedly beautiful black leathers. 'Cost me a grand.'

'So where does all the money come from? Not from Harry Lacon!'

'No, not from Harry.' He poured the rest of her beer into her glass. 'I have a couple of profitable sidelines in London.'

'Such as?'

'Them as asks no questions hears no lies.'

'Oh, *Ry*!' Her appetite fading, Ginny sat back to stare at him. 'You're not involved in . . .'

'In?' he prompted, watching her with a slightly wry expression.

'Something awful. Drugs. Or crime.'

He kept on looking at her for a long moment, and she felt herself go pale. She'd suddenly rediscovered just what a gaping void lay between Ry Savage and a man like Miles Langton. 'Oh, Ry,' she said again. 'Are you?'

His grin was sudden. 'What a horribly suspicious mind you have!'

'Then what is it? Ry, just tell me it isn't anything really ugly, and I won't ask another question, ever,' she pleaded.

'Does it mean that much to you?' he enquired.

'You know it does.'

'OK. It's not anything really ugly.' His voice and face were deadpan, and she had to be content with that. If he was lying to her . . . well, he was lying, and she could do nothing about it. How different Miles was from Ry! With Miles you never wondered. You never doubted his integrity, or his honesty, or his sense of responsibility. Ry might make Miles look pale in some respects, but when it came to the things that mattered, Miles was the better man, by a very long shot . . .

'You're right,' she sighed. 'This *is* a nice change.'

'The Willows is like a funeral parlour.'

'What would you know about it? It's not boiled hake and mash there, you know. It's asparagus soup and chicken à la King.'

'Same general colour scheme—pale and flaccid. I recognise Miles's taste. By the way, how did you get out of your luncheon date with the great man?'

'I didn't. Miles cancelled first.'

'Ah.' His lashes drooped. 'So I got you by default?'

She picked up her knife and fork, and giggled. The hot weather, hotter food, and two beers gulped down in quick succession were making her feel very full and rather giddy. 'You're still a troublemaker, aren't you?'

'Explain.'

'You're determined to say something about Miles that will really get my goat. But it won't work. I'm much too fond of him, and I can see right through you.'

'OK,' he invited, 'what does the label on the back of my T-shirt say?'

'It says Troublemaker. It says, "The person wearing me never had a stable home, so he pretends to despise all happy couples." '

Ry had stopped eating. He took a last swallow of beer, and sat back to watch her with slitted blue eyes. 'Go on. What else does it say?'

'It says you're wanton and destructive, and your main pleasure in life is causing trouble for other people. It also says you're madly jealous.'

'Of you?'

'Of every woman you've ever touched. You don't give a damn about any of them, yet you hate to see them find happiness with any other man. That shows up how empty your own life is, you see. So your instinct is to get in there and start destroying. That's what you're *really* good at.'

She, too, had finished, and she surveyed him with

slightly flushed cheeks. 'Sorry, Ry,' she said in a gentler tone, 'but you asked for that. You had no right to say the things you did about me and Miles.'

'Well, well.' His fingers were drumming slowly on the table, the only sign that she'd struck home. 'You *have* matured in the past year and a half! Matured, and developed a set of grown-up claws.'

For some reason, another pang of guilt, making her third that day, stabbed Ginny's heart.

'You can't deny that it's an accurate portrait of you,' she said defensively.

'It might have been accurate five or six years ago.' His eyes didn't leave hers. 'Doesn't it occur to you that I might have reformed?'

Ginny dropped her eyes to his unshaven jaw, then to his bronzed, bare chest. 'You?' she said derisively. 'Reformed? There's an old fable about the leopard changing his spots, Ry. The point being that it can't.'

'Or that people won't let it.' His voice was cool. 'You talk as though you almost don't want me to have changed.'

'Maybe I don't,' she smiled. 'I should be sorry to have you reformed and sanitised into something fit for a maiden's dream. It's rather nice to have a real bad boy in my dull little world. You add a touch of colour to the grey monotony, Ry.' She pulled herself up, realising that the alcohol was making her unwisely loquacious. 'However,' she added with more asperity, 'once every eighteen months is quite enough.' She glanced at her watch.

Ry followed her eyes. 'And is that my ration for the next eighteen months?' he asked.

'I'm afraid so,' Ginny nodded. 'I meant it. I've stopped waiting for you.' She checked her watch. 'My lunch-break ends at two.' She took a deep breath, knowing that what she had to say would be painful. 'Please don't come and see me again, Ry. If you'd been more mature this morning, more adult . . .' She shook her head. 'But you weren't. I'm serious about Miles, very serious. I can't afford to let anything compromise my engagement to him, not even you. Not even for old times' sake.'

'I see.' The beautifully rugged face was deadpan again, and his fingers had stopped drumming.

Ginny was congratulating herself on how well she was handling this situation. Better than she'd expected to, in fact. This was probably the first time in her life that she'd been able to deal with Ryan Savage in anything like an adult way. Certainly the first time she'd ever silenced him like this! She gave him a challenging look, as though daring him to argue.

'OK,' he said with a shrug of one shoulder.

Ginny felt her expression change. 'OK? You mean you aren't going to pester me—or anything like that?'

'Of course not,' Ry said easily. The perfect teeth glinted in a sabre-stroke of a smile. 'Why should I if you don't want me to? There are plenty of willing, buxom wenches over Newton way.'

'Oh.' She drew herself up stiffly and glared at him. 'Well, if *that's* all you wanted . . .'

His eyes noticed the outline of her breasts. 'What else should I want?'

'Well . . .' She felt the skin of her back prickle with heat, 'I knew your intentions were dishonourable, but not quite *that* dishonourable.'

'You thought I'd come along specifically to put a spoke in your wedding-carriage wheels?'

'That's the impression you gave,' she said, trying hard not to sound flat.

'No,' he said calmly. His blue eyes met hers innocently. 'Nothing so romantic. I just wanted a tumble in the hay.'

'You *what*?'

'I thought we'd stop off on the way home and find a sunny haystack. That's the local custom, you know.'

She was shocked, and didn't try to hide it. 'Ry!'

'Why so horrified?' he asked with a slight smile. 'You know I've been itching for you ever since you were sixteen.' He signalled to the waitress, then turned back to face her frozen expression. 'But marry Miles, if you must. I just thought I'd better have you before he did. The right man for the right job. I'd hate to think of it being bungled. Is that so wrong?'

'I ought to throw this plate at you,' she said through gritted teeth.

Ry laughed softly, his eyes dancing. 'Sweet little virgin,' he said softly, 'with sharp little claws. Have I touched a raw spot?'

'Can we go now, please?'

'Of course we can go. Your wish is my command.'

He paid for the meal with one of the fifties she'd given him that morning, and left a substantial tip for the waitress. Ginny followed him out into the bright sunlight, hardly pleased by the prospect of being forced to cling to him all the way back into town. What an idiot she'd been to go anywhere with him, and expose herself to that kind of hurt and humiliation.

'Here. Preserve the hairstyle for *cher* Miles.'

He fitted the helmet over her head, and strapped it under her chin. It smelled of his hair, clean and masculine. Ry lifted the plexiglass visor to speak to her.

'That was an odd reaction, by the way.'

'What was?' she asked shortly.

'Back there.' He nodded his curly head in the direction of the Cuban Hat. 'When you heard I hadn't come to prise you away from Miles. You looked quite disappointed.'

He kissed his finger, touched it to her nose, and flipped the visor back down over her startled face.

'You'll never guess in a million years who turned up in the bank yesterday morning, Mum.'

'Well, if it's someone that obscure, I suppose I never will,' Ginny's mother smiled, 'until you decide to tell me.'

'Ryan Savage.'

Her mother paused in laying the table, and glanced quickly at Ginny. 'Ry? What did he want?'

'To make trouble, what else?' Ginny grinned. 'I let him take me to the Cuban Hat for lunch.'

Prudence Northcliffe's eyebrows lifted in dismay. 'Oh, Ginny,' she sighed. 'It isn't something to be flippant about. You should be much more careful, love!'

'It was rather fun, actually.'

'You'd better tell me everything over tea,' her mother commanded firmly, and went to fetch the food.

They settled down to a late-afternoon tea in the sunny dining-room. Ginny and her mother had moved to White Cottage, with its limewashed walls and slated roof, soon after her father's death, over ten years ago. When Ginny had started working at the bank last year, a period which had coincided with the time her courtship with Miles started in earnest, she'd taken a bachelor flat in the middle of the town. The little cottage was just too far out from Grantley, while the flat was just around the corner from work; and as Ginny's mother had diplomatically pointed out, it gave Ginny more chance of a social life.

However, she still came to White Cottage to see her mother a couple of times a week, especially when—as today—her mother wanted help with some household job. As they ate, Ginny gave her an account of the afternoon with Ry at the Cuban Hat.

It was odd to think, on looking back, how well she'd handled Ry. That had been the first time she'd ever been able to control their relationship, be the one to dictate terms. Maybe it was a sign of her growing maturity, of the way she'd grown up since her engagement to Miles . . .

She'd been harsh with Ry. Maybe too harsh. She remembered her own words with a slight pang. *You're wanton and destructive, and your main pleasure in life is causing trouble for other people.* That had been unkind. But also true. And maybe it was time someone told Ry the truth about himself. He'd earned that rebuke, by trying to attack her engagement to Miles . . .

Prudence Northcliffe listened in an attentive silence as Ginny told the tale—leaving out a few minor details, like the way Ry had kissed her in the car park. Her expression was concerned. It was easy to see where Ginny had got her sweet face and graceful figure. Her mother was still absurdly youthful, an impression heightened by a slightly shy, diffident manner. Not even the touch of grey in her hair, which seemed to have increased since her husband's death, could contradict the freshness and lightness that seemed to surround her.

'I just hope,' she sighed, when Ginny had finished, 'that Miles doesn't get to hear about any of this. It wasn't exactly wise, Ginny. *Especially* to go to the Cuban Hat, of all places! Anybody might have seen you there, and it isn't a place with a very nice reputation.'

'I know. It was taking a chance.' Despite herself, Ginny was still smiling at the memory of that lunch. 'But, as I told you, I handled the situation without any problems. Anyway, what could I do? It would have been cruel to turn him down, when he'd come to see me especially. He's an old friend.'

'Only a friend?' her mother repeated, giving the word a slight emphasis.

'I'm not still infatuated with him, don't worry.' Ginny helped herself to more food. 'I grew out of my schoolgirl crush on Ry Savage a long time ago.' Her cheeks had pinkened slightly. She contemplated her plate intently. 'In fact, yesterday just helped to put it all in perspective again. I can't think why I ever thought he was so wonderful. You should have seen him, Mum, dressed like James Dean or someone, all in leather, and with a week's beard on his chin. So rough, so . . . primitive, almost. He couldn't be more different from Miles if he tried! I sat there wondering what I ever saw in him.'

'Did you?'

Ginny looked up. 'He doesn't even begin to compare with Miles.'

'It's not a question of comparisons,' her mother said, pouring more tea. 'It's a question of understanding your own heart.'

'Come on, Mum, you know me better than that. I'm getting married to Miles Langton in a few weeks!'

'Yes,' her mother nodded, chestnut hair glinting. 'Which is why you shouldn't still be seeing Ry Savage.'

'I'm not *seeing* him,' Ginny said with a flush of irritation. 'He just arrived out of the blue. If I'd refused to go out with him, it would have looked as though I still cared about him, which I definitely do not. It was more to say goodbye to him than anything else. To tell him how things stood between me and Miles, and to ask him not to ever bother me again.'

Her mother's eyes, a darker shade of brown than her own, searched her face with cool wisdom. 'And you say he's working at Newton for the summer?'

'Yes. But that doesn't mean he's going to keep pestering me, Mum. He got the message yesterday. I saw to that.'

'Ryan Savage has never been one to get a message he doesn't want to hear,' Prudence Northcliffe said with a touch of dryness. 'He's always done exactly as he chose, and I've lost count of the people who thought they'd managed to reorganise his life for him. They were always wrong.'

'Well, I know you disapprove of him . . .'

'I never said I disapproved of him,' her mother interrupted. 'But even if I did, that isn't the point, Ginny.'

'So what *is* the point?' Ginny invited uncomfortably.

'The point is that Ryan Savage used to dangle your

heart on a string,' her mother said with the forcefulness she sometimes unexpectedly commanded. 'You used to sit doodling hearts and writing his name millions of times in your sketchpads.'

'When I was sixteen!'

'Also when you were seventeen, eighteen, and nineteen, Ginny. Now you tell me he's back in the district, working a few miles away, and apparently intent on breaking up your engagement to Miles Langton. And then you sit there with that silly smug smile on your face, and tell me you're perfectly in control of the situation!'

Ginny squirmed. 'OK, OK, I get the message. If it's any consolation, I made him swear that he wouldn't come near me again. He'll stick to his word.'

Her mother sniffed. 'You've caged the tiger, have you?'

'Definitely,' Ginny said firmly. 'As for him breaking up my engagement—he doesn't have a hope, and he knows it. It just hurts when people assume I'm marrying for money. Why do they think it's so impossible to love someone twenty years older?'

'People are funny that way,' her mother said, without a single spark of irony in her wide hazel eyes.

'I *do* love Miles, you know. What I felt for Ry was just a teenage pash. It's over now. It's been over for nearly two years.'

'Well . . . I don't know about a teenage pash. You were once very keen to marry Ry.'

'Marry Ry?'

It was said with such scorn that her mother held up her hands in surrender. 'Very well, my love. I just hope for your sake that you know your own mind.'

'Of course I know my own mind!' Ginny gave her mother an indignant glare, which slowly melted into a rueful smile as her mother covered her ears in mock-pain. 'Sorry. Was I shouting?'

'Let's say you were protesting very loudly,' her mother

smiled, getting up to clear the table. 'Will you give me a hand with those curtains when we've washed up?'

Ginny was conscious of an uncomfortable feeling inside herself over the next half-hour. Her mother had a way of saying somewhat indigestible things, for all her light and innocent appearance. She was beginning to feel that she might not have been so clever yesterday, after all.

They unhooked the living-room curtains and spread them over the table to start the job of re-lining them. In the unfiltered light from the naked window, Ginny glanced round the cottage. As ever, it was as clean and neat as a new pin. Her mother wouldn't have dreamed of letting it get any other way. But it could in no sense be called a luxurious place. There were frayed edges, worn places, no trimmings of opulence. That Prudence Northcliffe wasn't a rich woman was patently obvious.

Even these curtains, being re-lined for their third lease of life, should really have been replaced with new ones long ago. In her father's day, they would have been. But his death had changed a lot of things.

Ginny had been just twelve when her father had died. She hadn't understood about debts and insurance and pension schemes then. But she'd understood that the financial and emotional security she'd always taken for granted had suddenly disappeared. She'd understood that her father's death had left her and her mother not just alone, but also poor.

Alone and poor. Two words which still filled her with an inner dread. The years of struggle had been dark and long, and she knew she would never really forget them. The big house in the village had been sold, and they'd moved here, with little more than the proceeds of the house-sale to live on. The little white cottage had seen a lot of self-sacrifice and a lot of renunciation in the years since then.

Mend and make do. A penny saved is a penny earned. Waste not, want not. Look after the pennies, and the pounds will look after themselves . . . A litany of frugal proverbs that had coloured her teenage years, years which had skirted the dreary borderline between thrift and hardship, as long as she could remember.

Her mother had worked hard to give her the best education she could afford, had struggled and sacrificed to give her security and comfort. And Ginny, in her turn, had done without so many of the little luxuries that girls of her age took for granted. She'd learned long ago to put practical, essential things first, and never to waste money on anything frivolous.

It had only been in the past few years, since she'd finished her education, and had started working, that a touch of ease had entered their lives. She'd been able to start paying her mother back in little ways, though it was hard to get Mum to accept anything. Ginny sometimes wondered whether her mother would ever really learn to forget the habit of scrimping and saving.

Marry Ry? Not in a million years. She wasn't going to throw all that carefully built-up achievement away on a man who was fundamentally unable to take care of her!

No amount of surface attraction to Ry Savage could dispel that deep, pragmatic knowledge that he just wasn't responsible. He would never make anyone a good husband. By the same token, it was unlikely that he could ever make any child a good father, either. And she didn't want any child of hers to have to go through what she and her mother had gone through . . .

They unpicked the faded old lining, and set up the sewing-machine to stitch the new material in. The old lining was starting to perish, but Ginny knew better than to throw it away. It would come in handy for something, her mother would see to that. Nothing went to waste in White Cottage.

There was a warm feeling in knowing that her marriage to Miles Langton was going to make a substantial difference to her mother's life. Looking round the room, she was, unsuspected by her mother, already redecorating White Cottage, and refurnishing it with lovely new things and pretty new materials, making it warm and cosy and snug.

It gave her a great deal of satisfaction to think of what she was going to be able to do for Mum. Miles, of course, knew exactly what her mother's situation was, and had promised practical, financial help. That sort of kindness was typical of Miles's generous heart.

Not that her mother had any idea of what was planned. She would have been offended if she had. And when Miles did start helping, it would have to be done tactfully, or her mother's pride would be painfully hurt. But ever since her girlhood, she had ached to make her mother's life easier, and her marriage to Miles Langton was going to enable her to do just that.

'What was that proverb Grandma always used to recite?' she asked, feeding the hem under the whirring foot of the old Singer. 'Something about a rich man's darling?'

'"Better a rich man's darling than a poor man's slave",' her mother quoted. An odd expression crossed her face. 'I haven't heard that saying for ages. I wonder whether there's really any truth in it . . . I wouldn't like to think that you were marrying for no better reason than to be a rich man's darling!'

'Of course I'm not,' Ginny said emphatically, keeping her eye on the hem. 'Don't be silly.'

'A poor man's slave,' her mother mused. 'She meant Daddy, of course. She never approved of my marrying your father. She used to say he'd never make a good provider.'

'Well, she was right, wasn't she?' Ginny enquired. 'I mean, Daddy was lovely, but he wasn't really responsible. And he left things in such a mess when he died . . .'

'Oh, yes, he wasn't a practical man. I was being courted by other young men, you know, with much better prospects in life. You could tell that they would go a long way. Or at least, a much longer way than your father ever would.' She glanced up with soft brown eyes. 'But I was happy with him, Ginny. I never regretted my choice. I married for love.'

Ginny gave a prickly little shrug. 'I'm also marrying for love, Mum. Do I have to swear an oath?'

'I never said you weren't,' her mother smiled. 'My, my! Ryan Savage really seems to have got under your skin.'

'He always does,' Ginny sighed. 'He *always* does. Right, that's one finished. Let's do the other.'

They dropped the subject by unspoken agreement, and spent the rest of the afternoon in gossip of a more idle nature.

But Ginny's thoughts stayed with Ry, and a part of her mind kept returning to yesterday lunch time.

It had been so good to see him again, logic or no logic. God, but she had missed him! Something had gone out of her life when Ry had left Grantley, something bright and exciting which she couldn't put a finger on. Youth, maybe? Whatever it was, for a long, long while she'd been bereft without him. Mum had been right. She'd been a heart on a string, and when Ry let the string go, she would just plummet . . .

He had never had the slightest concern for her feelings. In fact, Ryan Savage had never taken her seriously at all.

Whereas Miles Langton had always taken her very seriously indeed. Miles cared what she felt, listened to her, gave her reassurance. Ry, on the other hand, was a mocker. She could never talk seriously to him, because he would tease her into giggles, or laugh her to shame. Ry would never let her get away with the slightest bit of pretence or pretension. With Miles, she always felt adult, respected.

She'd summed it up perfectly when she'd told Ry at the Cuban Hat, *He treats me like a lady.* No man could ever understand what that meant, least of all a nonconformist like Ry.

It had taken Miles Langton's wooing to remind her that she was worth something, after all; to teach her that she was valuable, and cherished, and to give her direction again. The realisation of how deeply Miles cared for her had opened an unsuspected new horizon in her life. Her feelings about Ryan Savage had suddenly fallen into perspective.

She had finally found someone who loved her, who really loved her in a mature way. Someone who was prepared to stay at her side. Someone who didn't rush away from her whenever he grew bored. Someone who would treasure her, who would form a family with her, and who would give her the old-fashioned, cast-iron security she ached for. The fact that he was rich didn't really enter into it.

It had never troubled her that her feelings for Miles Langton were not of the lurid, illustrated-magazine kind. She had finally grown out of such dreams.

Their love was of a deeper, stronger nature. It showed less on the surface, but that was because it was strong and dependable deep down, where it counted. Whereas what she felt for Ry had always been a skin-deep thing, an excitement that was without any meaningful depths. He would never provide the kind of trust that Miles could, she knew that.

And having faced that, she knew that the illusions she'd once had about Ry Savage would never return.

CHAPTER THREE

'COME ON, Lucy.' Ginny turned and beckoned to the child. 'You can't pick every flower on the riverbank.'

'I need some more daisies,' Lucy said importantly. 'I'm making a boo-kay.' She squatted in the dappled sunlight, concentrating on the co-ordination needed to pick daisies with one hand while clutching a tattered 'boo-kay' in the other. Ginny smiled. She loved children in any case, but Lucy, her cousin Alison Wentworth's five-year-old, was particularly adorable. She was going to be the only flower-girl at her own wedding in a few weeks time, and since being told of this signal honour, had developed a passionate interest in flowers.

She checked her watch. Lucy wasn't due for her dinner until six, and it really was so beautiful here . . . She found a handy bench, and sat down to watch the little girl playing.

It was one of those rare, roastingly hot summer days, when the river was about the only place you could find a cool breeze. The paved walk was crowded with people walking or cycling in bright summer clothes, and upstream, boys were swimming in the water. Strictly illegally, of course. But she herself had done the same thing at their age, on just such afternoons as this.

Despite her crisp cotton sundress, Ginny was hot enough to feel sticky. Listening to the splashing and shrieking of the children, she eyed the water longingly, and wished she was fourteen again. But she wasn't. The days when she and Ry had paddled in the cool water together were long gone. She sighed, leaning back and letting the warmth of the sun wash over her.

Lucy gave a little cry as some of the flowers escaped her clumsy fingers, and raised a woebegone face to Ginny.

'I've *dropped* um!'

'Let me help.' She went over to the child, and knelt beside her in the grass. 'You've picked them too short,' she said as she started rescuing the flowers. 'You have to pick them longer than that, Lucy, or they won't even stick over the top of the vase.'

'Is that long enough?' Lucy enquired, holding up a sprig of purple clover.

'That's better,' Ginny nodded. She solemnly presented Lucy with the flowers, thinking how lovely the child was going to look at her wedding.

It was her dream to have a little girl like this. Or a little boy, she wasn't fussy. Having children, in fact, had been a major factor in Ginny's decision to accept Miles.

She and Miles were planning to start a family quite soon after their wedding; given Miles's age, it was important that they have them without delay, and that suited her too. She wanted children of her own, with growing urgency. Children would seal the ring of safety she intended to build around herself.

She took Lucy's free hand. 'Come, love. You've got enough now. Leave some for other people to enjoy.'

They rejoined the path, hand in hand, the child prattling happily about the wedding that was to be. Her notions of the part she was to play were rather vague, but she knew she was going to be an important figure in the ceremony.

As they walked up towards the village, Ginny was aware of the whirr of a bicycle behind them. She moved to the edge of the path to let it pass, but the cyclist slowed and stopped, and a familiar voice said, 'Well, well, what a pretty picture!'

She spun round, knowing it was Ry. He was leaning on the handlebars of the bicycle, smiling at her lazily, naked to the waist, wearing only denims and trainers, his magnificent body gleaming in the sun like bronze.

'How did you know I would be here?' Ginny demanded, slightly breathlessly.

'Don't you believe in coincidence?' he grinned, bright blue eyes dancing.

'Not where you're concerned.' She surveyed him with a jaundiced eye. 'Showing off your manly physique?'

'It's too hot for a shirt. The BMW's in the garage for a new piston, and this was all I could borrow at the farm. I've just cycled all the way from Newton, and there isn't even a pub on the route.' He nodded his dark head at the river. 'Remember when we used to swim there on summer's days like this?'

'I was just thinking about that,' she confessed. Her heart was still pounding inside her, reacting to the undeniable excitement of seeing him again.

Whatever else he might be, Ry had a beautiful body, as beautiful as an ancient Greek athlete's in some marvellous statue. The powerful muscles were sharply defined under the silky skin, tapering from wide, formidable shoulders to a lithe waist, the total lack of fat testifying to long, gruelling hours of exercise. His jeans were tight enough to reveal that the rest of his body was equally hard and potent. Crisp dark hair spread across his chest, trickling down his flat belly into his waistband, giving him a pagan, almost primitive look.

As he swung himself off the bicycle, it was like watching a statue come to magical life, the tendons and muscles working in fluid harmony.

He bent down to Lucy, who had been gaping at him, open-mouthed with awe. 'And who,' he enquired with a smile, 'is this young lady?'

'This is Lucy,' Ginny said. 'My cousin Alison's daughter. I was just taking her for a stroll before tea.'

'Hello, Lucy.' Ry reached out and swung the little girl effortlessly into his arms. He tucked her against his naked side, looking at her solemnly. 'My name is Ryan, and I'm a very, very wicked man.'

'Hello,' said Lucy in a small voice, her eyes huge.

'What a beautiful bunch of flowers,' Ry smiled. 'Daisies and clover and buttercups. Who are they for?'

'Me.' Lucy pondered for a moment, looking as pretty as a flower herself in Ry's strong, tanned arms. Then she put the bunch forward. 'But you can have um.'

'I don't want um,' Ry grinned. 'You'll have more use for them, gorgeous.'

Ginny was watching in silence, but her heart was aching with a fierce pang. The dark-haired, blue-eyed Lucy might easily have been his daughter. How beautiful he was, with the child in his arms! So handsome, so tall and straight, like something out of a storybook about the way things should be, but never were in real life.

With something like grief, she was thinking what a wonderful father Ry would make. Would he ever settle down, and marry some lucky girl, and produce a brood of beautiful, healthy children? The thought was unbearably painful for some reason, and she felt her throat choke up with emotion.

Lucy was giggling with delight now. Ry had hoisted her up to the dizzy height of his shoulders, and she was clinging to his neck, her bouquet discarded and forgotten. Ry reached for Ginny's hand. 'You're not in any hurry, are you?'

'Lucy has to have her dinner . . .' But she was taking his hand, all the same, feeling his strong fingers lace through hers. 'I can't stay long, Ry.'

'Oh, take that better-judgement look off your face,' he commanded. 'I'm not contagious, you know. You can talk to me for a few minutes without danger.'

The walked down to the river's edge and stood looking across at the other bank. Almost, she thought, with that same odd pain in her heart, like a real family. Ry's half-naked body was close beside her. She could feel his warmth, smell the healthy musk of his skin. 'It's beautiful, isn't it,' he sighed, his eyes dreamy. 'Living in London, you dream of days like this and scenes like this.

You're very lucky to have it all, Ginny.'

'And you're very lucky to have the excitement of London,' she said drily. 'It's easy to be sentimental about the idyllic countryside. But day-to-day life in Grantley isn't exactly thrilling.'

'It has its compensations.' Ry lowered the now-sleepy Lucy, and cradled her in his arms, so that her flushed face rested against his bare chest. As always, she reflected wryly, he had found no difficulty in conquering a female heart, even a five-year-old one. He turned to Ginny with a half-smile. 'Anyway, you should be the last person to feel bored, Ginny darling. On the eve of your wonderful, exciting marriage to wonderful, exciting Miles Langton.'

'Is that meant to be funny?'

'It's rather tragic, actually.' He was stroking Lucy's hair absently. 'It's always tragic to see someone you care for throwing themselves away.'

'And I suppose you've done wonderful things with *your* life?' she said spitefully.

'We were talking about you,' he reproved gently, 'not me.'

'And what gives you the right to be so proprietorial?' Ginny looked up into his face challengingly. The face she'd seen so often in her dreams, with its wide, sexy mouth and deep blue eyes, the thick black hair curling almost to his shoulders.

'Maybe nothing. But do you realise what a permanent step marriage is? It's very easy to get into, but not so easy to get out of. And it's impossible to get out of it without a lot of scars and pain.'

'I'm not a child, Ry,' she said in a clipped voice. 'I know exactly how serious marriage is.'

'Do you? You've got a kind of blind look in your eyes these days. As though you don't want to see what's really happening to you.' Lucy was by now fast asleep against his shoulder, and Ry kissed the child's temple almost absently. 'It isn't too late to cancel everything, you know.'

'Just because you tell me to?' she said tightly. Unhappy anger was starting to ball inside her. 'You've got a nerve, Ry!'

He glanced at her with vivid eyes. 'I can't believe you really love that man, Ginny darling.'

'Can't you?' Ginny retorted with a dangerous sparkle. 'Well, I do!'

'It's impossible.'

'That sounds like colossal vanity to me.'

'What's vanity got to do with it?'

'Plenty. You're so used to having me mooning over *you* that it wounds your male pride to see me care for another man!'

'Well, it's true I fancy you pretty desperately,' he smiled. 'I always have done. But that isn't the reason I'm worried about you. If I thought you loved Miles——'

'What do you know about love, anyway?' she snapped, tight with anger. 'Since when are you the great expert on human relationships?'

'Oh, I forgot,' he said wryly. 'I never had a stable home, so I despise all happy couples. I'm wanton and destructive, and I like causing trouble for other people. Have I quoted accurately?' Ginny dropped her eyes, her cheeks colouring. 'For all that,' he went on softly, 'I'm older than you, and I care about you pretty deeply—for a wanton, destructive troublemaker. It isn't jealousy speaking, Ginny.' He smiled slightly. 'Or not just jealousy, at any rate.' His arm slid round her waist like a python, pulling her close against him, and her heart twisted at the contact with his warm, naked skin. 'You should listen to me,' he said huskily.

'And you want me to believe you've reformed?' She pulled away from him bitterly, and reached out to take Lucy from his arms. 'I've got to go, Ry.'

'Why won't you talk about it?'

'It's too late for talk. I love Miles, and I'm going to

marry him. And now it's time for Lucy's dinner!'

'Blind. Quite blind.' With a sigh, he passed the sleepy little girl back to her.

She propped Lucy on her hip and gave Ry a last glare. 'You said you weren't going to pester me, Ry. And I *don't* believe in coincidence where you're concerned. Stay away from me in future.'

'You're beautiful when you're angry.' His eyes did a slow up-down survey of her figure, lit by the hot golden sunlight. 'And you look gorgeous with that kid in your arms,' he added huskily, his eyes hooded. 'Sure you won't run away with me to the Fiji Islands?'

'We wouldn't get very far on your bicycle,' she said sourly, and turned to go. She walked up the riverbank and on to the path, her nerves still tingling with resentment at the things he'd said to her. What gave him the *right* to treat her like his personal property?

At the top of the path, she turned and glanced over her shoulder. Ry was still standing by the river, watching her leave. His muscular arms were folded, and his face wore that same brooding expression.

Angrily she turned without waving, and headed back up the river-walk towards Alison's house.

Miles's courtship had been like everything else he did—slow, sure, and very careful. So careful, in fact, that when they publicly announced their engagement, all her friends, and most of his, had been utterly taken aback.

That was probably why, even though they'd been courting for nearly two years, Ginny had fielded a lot of very dry looks coming her way since the brief announcement in the *Post.* No one had been quite as blunt about their suspicions as Ry Savage, of course, but people had managed to get the message across, all the same. A pretty young girl with no money, a middle-aged bachelor with plenty: the inference was there for anyone with that sort of mind.

Some people, mainly women in Miles's age-group, were obvious about it. The cool snubs, expertly delivered, the casual emphasis that turned an otherwise harmless sentence into an insult, Ginny had faced them all.

Others were much more subtle about it. They never said or did anything that was direct; the message was conveyed by the elaborate politeness with which they treated her, that knowing look in their eyes.

One such was Dodie Witherburn.

'Oh, money will make *such* a difference to your life,' she cooed, meaning Miles's money. 'I'm sure you've thought of that.'

'It had crossed my mind.'

'It's not just the money, of course. You'll have a *position* in Grantley. Position makes a great deal of difference to one's life. That's the point of this story I'm telling. Are you *sure* you won't have another gin and tonic, by the way? You must never be shy with us, you know. We're Miles's oldest friends. If you can't feel at home with *us*, then who *can* you feel at home with?' Her thin mouth smiled while her pale grey eyes stared fishily.

'It's too hot for alcohol,' Ginny smiled. She slithered down in the deck-chair and fanned herself with her straw hat. The ritual Saturday-afternoon drinking at the Witherburns' could be stupefying. 'Much too hot!'

'Gina says it's much too hot for alcohol,' Dodie trilled to the men, as though the remark had been some rare witticism. Miles and Edward were sitting a little way apart on the bowling-green lawn that was the Witherburns' pride and joy. They didn't interrupt the low murmur of their conversation to answer the inane comment.

'Go on with your story,' Ginny invited. 'What happened then?'

'Well,' said Dodie, mixing herself another gin, '*then* I said, look here, young man, it's Mrs Edward Witherburn speaking . . .'

Dodie liked to call herself Mrs Edward Witherburn. That was in case anyone had forgotten that her husband was the second most respected man in Grantley.

Edward Witherburn, whom Ginny liked far better than his colourless and cold-eyed wife, was in many ways a shadow-copy of Miles. Edward was vice-chairman of the local Rotary Club, deputy secretary of the golf club, and sub-treasurer of the Country Club. He was the sort of boring, pleasant, self-satisfied man whom it was very hard to dislike, and he seemed more than content to play second fiddle to Miles Langton for the rest of his days.

That, effectively, paired Ginny off with Dodie. And Dodie was still trying to swallow the prospect of playing second lady of Grantley to a woman half her age and twice as pretty as she had ever been.

'. . . he was a *little* before your time, but I'm sure you remember him,' Dodie said, tinkling the ice musically in her glass. As was her way, one story had blurred illogically but imperceptibly into another. 'He had the big house on Forest Road, with the three gables.'

'No,' Ginny said apologetically, 'I'm sorry, I don't remember him.'

'*Don't* you?' The places where Dodie's eyebrows would have been, if she hadn't plucked every last hair, rose upwards. 'But surely. No, *surely.* Such a lovely man. Well, let me see. He died just after the new hospital was built, and that was . . . how silly of me!' she gushed. 'You were just a *baby* at the time. How *could* you have remembered him?'

'Yes,' Ginny smiled a little glassily, 'how could I have remembered him?'

'How *silly* of me.' Dodie gave a little shriek of laughter that sounded like pain, and turned to the men again. 'I've just asked Gina if she remembers Jim Wentworth. Jim *Wentworth.* I mean, she was just a *baby* when he died . . .'

It was with a blessed sense of relief that Ginny finally climbed into Miles's Jaguar and waved goodbye to the

Witherburns in the late afternoon.

Setting off home at his regulation thirty miles an hour, Miles gave her a slight smile. 'How was your afternoon?'

'Deadly,' Ginny said succinctly.

'That bad?'

'The same as always.' She sighed. 'If only she were just plain boring, I wouldn't mind. When is she going to stop being so *amazed* at how young I am?' She imitated Dodie's whinny. ' "I mean, she was just a *baby* when he died." ' It starts to wear thin after a while, Miles.'

'She doesn't mean any harm.'

'Oh, yes, she does. She just doesn't have the courage to inflict it. An afternoon with Dodie is like being attacked by a shoal of toothless piranhas.'

Miles looked amused, but only for a moment. He was wearing tailored slacks and a sports jacket, with a navy blue scarf at his throat; a well-polished pair of brogues and a just-alight pipe completed his weekend attire. Ginny had never seen him in anything more casual than that. 'I'm sorry you find them quite so dull,' he said regretfully. 'They're among my best friends, as you know.'

'Oh, I like Edward. I think he likes me too. But Dodie is never going to accept me. Nibble, nibble, nibble. Have you seen her eyes when she looks at me? And that laugh! It's like someone stepping on a toy poodle. She only does it when I'm around. She thinks I'm after your money, Miles, and nothing is ever going to change her mind about that.'

Miles sucked at his pipe reflectively, then held it up to study the contents. He wasn't really a smoker; he used the paraphernalia of pipe scraping, stuffing, lighting and puffing as a way of steadying his thoughts. 'There are a number of people who have the same idea,' he said, and the slow way he said it let her know he'd been preparing this for some time. 'I know it must annoy you, but in a way, you can't blame them.'

'It hurts me, rather than annoys me,' Ginny said. 'And why shouldn't I blame them for such an unkind, unfair assumption?'

'Because they're only being realistic,' he replied, re-inserting the pipe. 'After all, I'm marrying a young and beautiful employee, and that always makes talk. Unequal marriages are often based on money. When you get to my age, you'll start realising just how mercenary the world really is. The only way you'll ever prove people wrong is by staying happily married to me for the rest of your life!'

She turned in the leather seat to face him, frowning. 'Doesn't it annoy you that people think of me as a mercenary little thing with no scruples?'

'No. I keep it in perspective.'

'So I've noticed. You're not exactly quick to defend me from these hags. Do reveal the secret,' Ginny prompted.

'I take it as something of a compliment, actually,' Miles said with a slight smile.

'How could it possibly be a compliment?'

'It shows that people care about me. They're concerned about my happiness, and they don't want to see me make a bad mistake. Their suspicion of you is just the natural caution of people who've been my friends for a long, long time.'

'I see,' Ginny said drily, thinking it over. Nice for him, but not so nice for her. 'I hadn't realised that you took it all as a personal tribute to your popularity in Grantley, Miles.'

'That wasn't what I said.'

'It's easy for *you* to take it in your stride,' she went on with a touch of bitterness. 'It isn't directed at you. As it happens, my feelings about you are very strong and sincere, and money doesn't enter into them. It upsets me very much that a contingent of your friends should feel otherwise, and that you don't make an effort to contradict them!'

'My friends are old enough to make their own minds

up,' he said, lips moving around the stem of the pipe. 'As I said, it's up to you to show them they're wrong.'

'And how long will that take?' she asked pointedly. 'Twenty years of being a faithful wife? By which time I'll be too jaded to care, and half of them will be senile, anyway.'

In the icy silence that followed, Ginny cursed herself briskly. That had *not* been a clever or diplomatic remark.

'I'm sorry,' she said quietly. 'That was a stupid thing to say.'

'Oh, forget it. I don't intend to be senile by the age of sixty-six,' said Miles. But there was no smile to warm the reply up. 'Don't forget,' he went on drily, 'that I've had to put up with a lot of nasty, snide comments from *your* friends.' For a moment his knuckles whitened on the wheel. 'If you remember, they were equally suspicious of me. It's hardly pleasant to be treated like some kind of old monster.'

'Yes, I know,' Ginny said with a pang of sympathy. 'But we don't see any of them any more. And we're going to be seeing your friends for a long, long time. It would mean a lot to me if you'd just take my part for once . . .'

He didn't reply as her voice tailed off, and for the next few minutes they sat without speaking. Ginny, for her part, was thoroughly miserable.

Eventually, Miles reached across and laid his hand over hers. 'Be realistic, Ginny,' he sighed. 'It isn't going to stop, not even after we're married. It's up to you to prove to them what a genuine person you are. You're too sensitive. Grow an extra skin until it all settles down.'

'I wish I could.' She thought back to the things Ry had said, that cynical look in his eyes. 'But what if they're right, after all?' she asked with a touch of anguish.

Miles chuckled. 'Of course they're not right. You've just said so. You're about the least mercenary person I know.'

That wasn't what she'd meant, but what she had meant

was too complex to go into now.

What she had meant was that her motives for agreeing to marry Miles Langton might be pragmatic, after all. Not that his wealth interested her. No, it had been Ry who'd put his finger on it: *what some girls will do for security!* She was hungry for the protection of a secure marriage. She'd always been. Yet wasn't that, in its way, as dangerous a motive as marrying for money? The idea of marrying someone for something other than love left a bad taste in the mouth. Or was that foolish idealism? It didn't matter, anyway, she told herself briskly. She *did* love Miles Langton, and she *didn't* love anyone else. So whatever else came with the marriage should be welcomed, as part of Miles's world. Miles was so good, so kind, so responsible. She ought to trust him more. That was probably the key to everything.

'I'm sorry I was so horrible about Dodie,' she said with a flash of contrition. 'She really isn't that bad. I'm going try a great deal harder next time, I promise.'

'That would mean a lot to me,' Miles said gently.

'I love you,' she sighed, leaning her head on his shoulder. 'You're so patient with me . . .'

'Don't be silly. And I love you too. I'm going to drop you off at your flat,' Miles volunteered, and she gave him a grateful smile. Saturdays usually ended with an evening at Greenlawns, Miles's big house on the river, where he lived with his sister Jessica.

Jessica was a few years older than Miles, a retired maths teacher. She was a still-handsome spinster who had been badly disappointed in love several years ago, and who had never repeated the experiment.

She and Ginny got on well, probably because Ginny had never tried to challenge her position in Miles's household. Miles was closer to Jessica than to anyone else; but he must have rightly guessed that Ginny had had her fill of middle-aged company for this particular Saturday.

'Don't forget we're going to the Country Club

tomorrow afternoon,' Miles reminded her as he pulled up outside the entrance to the little courtyard where she'd taken a flat.

She nodded, and gave him a quick kiss—Miles hated to be seen in public demonstrations of affection with her. 'Sorry about being such a drip today,' she said. 'It must be the heat. It always makes me jumpy. I'll be better tomorrow, I promise.'

'Just be as you always are.' He reached across her to open the door for her, and she waved the big silver Jaguar goodbye, then turned and walked under the stone archway into the square courtyard. The building had originally been a stables in the middle of the little town, but a few years ago an enterprising architect had converted it into three separate flatlets, sharing the charming cobbled yard. The tenants, all young people of Ginny's age-group, had put pots of geraniums and roses in the yard, and it was filled with scent and flowers.

But it was not the rustic beauty of the scene that made Ginny stop dead as she came through the archway.

It was the big black BMW motorcycle parked in the centre of the yard.

Her heart skipped a beat, and for an instant she was ready to turn back and run. Ry had given his word not to pursue her, damn him!

There was no sign of Ry himself, but her neighbour's door was slightly ajar, and Ginny smiled a sour little smile. No doubt Margaret Easy, perpetually man-hungry, and not shy about it, had let Ry into her flat, and was right now having the time of her life.

With a sigh in which resignation and anger were mixed, Ginny started forward again, and poked her head round Margaret's door.

The scene was just as she'd expected. As usual, Margaret's flat was on the borderline of slovenliness. Ry, wearing a deep red top this time, together with thigh-hugging denims that made no secret of his masculinity, was reclining in an armchair with his feet up. In one hand was a can of beer.

While Margaret was curled up on the settee opposite, talking with such animation that she couldn't possibly have noticed how her skirt had ridden up to expose the whole of one shapely thigh to Ry's heavy-lidded gaze.

'Oh, *hi,*' Margaret carolled as she spotted Ginny. She fluttered thick lashes. 'I've been entertaining your friend until you got back. Where *have* you been, love?'

'Where I always am on Saturdays,' Ginny said drily. 'You know I'm not usually back until late.'

'Oh my, I'd *absolutely* forgotten,' Margaret laughed, totally unabashed. 'Poor Ry might have had a long, long wait if you hadn't got home early for once. So what happened? No argument with dear Miles, I hope?'

'Nothing like that.' She gave Ry the same dry look. 'I'm going to make a snack and some coffee. Care to join me?'

'I don't know,' purred Ry. 'The view is rather pleasant right here.'

Margaret giggled, and shifted herself to reveal even more thigh, something Ginny would have thought impossible.

'In that case,' Ginny snapped, 'I'll just leave you to it. Goodnight.'

'Hold on!' Ry powered himself on to his feet with smooth grace. 'Don't go off like a bear-trap, Ginny.' He crumpled the beercan as though it had been a paper cup, and dropped it into a waste-basket. 'Thanks for the company, Margaret. I've enjoyed meeting you.'

Margaret uncoiled and gave Ry a big smile as she handed him his tan leather jacket. Somehow, the way she smoothed her T-shirt down made it look for a moment as though she were caressing her own heavy breasts. 'Any time,' she said huskily. And it was patently obvious that she meant *any time.*

Ry grinned, and it didn't improve Ginny's boiling temper that he wrapped a steel-strong arm possessively round her waist as they walked out.

'Nice girl, that,' he mused innocently.

'Get your paw off me, you—you *bear*!' she gritted. 'What are you doing here, anyway?'

'Oh, just passing through.'

'Well, next time, don't pass through Margaret's flat.' He was obviously still looking for that tumble in the hay, and if she hadn't got back early, he would certainly have been sampling Margaret's blonde charms by evening. He didn't have any morals, not a shred of decency, and nor did Margaret. Fancy trying to pretend she didn't know where Ginny was! Her fingers were unaccountably clumsy as she fumbled with the lock of her own front door, and Ry leaned over to kiss the sensitive skin behind her ear.

'You aren't supposed to be jealous of me,' he said huskily, his mouth tormentingly close to her ear.

'I'm not,' she snapped, and finally got the door open. 'I'm warning you for your own good!'

'I felt rather sorry for her. She told me she'd lost her job a couple of months ago.'

'Yes. Not too bothered about it, is she? And somehow she still has plenty to spend. That girl is *notorious*. Know what her surname is?'

'Surprise me.'

'Easy. Margaret Easy.'

'That seems very appropriate. She seemed such a warm, sweet person,' Ry said with another irreproachable face.

'Warm and sweet like a jar of molasses, set out to trap flies,' she retorted. 'And you look about as innocent as Mephistopheles, so give it up.'

Ry grinned. He was clean-shaven today, and his long black hair, tumbling almost to his broad shoulders, gave him the look of a Red Indian prince. With its wide sleeves and deep colour, the red top emphasised his muscular fitness as he slowly turned on one heel, hands on hips.

'Well, well!' Ry gazed admiringly round the flat. 'This is something else. Did *cher* Miles set you up in this little love-nest? It certainly makes Margaret's place look like a pigsty.'

'Miles did *not* set me up, and this is *not* a love-nest,' she said briskly. 'And you seemed to be having a whale of a time in Margaret's armchair, swilling her beer and looking up her skirt.'

'I love you when you get angry.' His hands had found the tops of her shoulders, and were massaging the tense muscles with soothing expertise. He was, she thought numbly, the sexiest man she would ever see. He drew her close as her tense neck sagged a little, and wrapped his arms round her waist.

She felt herself pulled up against his hard stomach, the length of his strong thighs unashamed against hers.

'What *have* you been doing with your beloved all this lovely summer afternoon?' he asked softly, looking down at her with those ocean-deep eyes.

'Visiting some boring people,' she said, trying to sound unaffected by his closeness. 'Let me go, please.'

'You mean there are people in Grantley even more boring than Miles?'

'Don't start,' she warned him, her flushed face raised challengingly to his. She put her hands on his arms to try and wrest them loose. They were iron-hard with muscle, but warm, and satin-skinned, and he merely smiled gently, his eyes studying the full oval of her mouth.

'Going somewhere?'

'To the kitchen. I'm hungry.'

'So am I,' he whispered. His mouth closed on hers with a little groan of appreciation, the kiss pressing insistently on her soft lips until they parted moistly, and Ginny stopped trying to push him away, her head spinning, and her heart pounding in her breast.

CHAPTER FOUR

WHY WAS IT that every feeling she had about Ry should be turned on its head when he kissed her? To be held against his big, warm body like this, to be kissed like this, made her melt like butter in the sun.

It was the *way* he held her, the *way* he kissed her. Miles kissed her with cool lips, careful not to hurt or offend in any way. Ry kissed her as though he were thinking of nothing else in the universe, as though she were the most important, most delicious, most overwhelming fact in his existence . . .

With a gasp, Ginny pulled away from him just as his tongue had started to explore her mouth, and all but ran to the kitchen. Ry followed, his eyes a deep smoky violet.

'You taste of gin and tonic,' he said, watching her fumble in the fridge. 'Very upper-classy.'

'And you taste of Margaret's beer,' she said, avoiding his eyes as she produced eggs, bacon and a box of mushrooms. 'I told you not to kiss me again.'

'I can't help it.' He folded his arms and leaned against the doorway. 'I look at that big, luscious mouth of yours and—wham! It happens all over again.'

'Extremely plausible.' Her hands were shaking as she started frying the bacon and mushrooms. That kiss had left her feeling very strange, filled with a sweet warmth, and yet aware that tears were not far beneath the surface. 'What are you doing this for, Ry? I thought I'd made everything clear at the Cuban Hat.'

'Clear to which of us? Me or you?'

'I don't intend to let you spoil things between me and Miles,' she said, looking up at him at last, her eyes dark.

'You have no right to. Perhaps you think it's a game to arrive here after almost two years and suddenly start paying me this kind of court, just to drive a wedge between me and Miles. Well, it isn't a game at all. It's wanton and destructive.'

'Is that really the way it seems to you?'

'Don't be a hypocrite,' she said acidly, and poked at the bacon. 'You don't really give a damn about me. You're just after the fun of spoiling something you can't have.'

'Would it make a difference if I *did* give a damn about you?' he asked gently.

'I know you too well for that,' she reminded him. 'Your pride has been piqued because you haven't found me waiting patiently for you, like faithful Fido.' Her brown eyes glinted. 'You'd like to prove your male magnetism, by getting me away from Miles. Just to show you could do it. The trouble is, you wouldn't have the slightest use for me once you'd got me!'

'Oh,' he purred, 'I could think of one or two things you'd be good for.'

She didn't dignify that with an answer. 'How many eggs can you eat?' she asked, pulling the bowl closer.

'All of them.' He moved up behind her as she started cracking them, and took her in his arms again, nuzzling his face into her fragrant chestnut hair. 'As it happens, I give rather more than a damn about you,' he said gently.

'I can't cook with you holding me like this,' she protested, threatening him with the spatula.

'You've always mattered to me. And I really do wish you'd waited for me.'

'I'd still have been waiting by Doomsday!'

'No, you wouldn't. I'd have been ready by then.' He kissed the side of her neck, then released her, and started opening drawers. 'Where do you keep the cutlery?'

'In there.' She looked over her shoulder at him. 'Is that why I only see you once every eighteen months? Because you care so much about me? Pull the other one, Ry!'

'I've been away for a long time, yes. But that doesn't mean I never think about you. I think about you all the time.' It was said with such simplicity that she almost believed him. 'You're always there, somewhere in my mind. I can't get you out of my thoughts, and I don't want to try. That's why I came to see you.' He laid the table neatly, moving around as though the flat were already completely familiar to him. 'As for my not wanting you to marry Miles Langton,' he went on, 'that is almost a separate issue.'

'A separate issue from what?' she said sceptically.

'From the fact that you're the only girl I've ever really wanted to bed,' he grinned.

Ginny flushed. 'That's only because you've already bedded all the rest,' she replied tersely.

'Maybe,' Ry nodded. 'But your marrying Miles Langton would be a horrible mistake.'

There was a photograph of Miles on the mantelpiece. She had taken the picture herself a few months ago, and Miles had bought her the silver frame to put it in.

Ry picked up the picture now, and studied it. 'He's not just old enough to be your father. He's a cold, selfish, calculating man who'll never give you a tenth of the love you need.'

'Ry, *stop!*' she warned him fiercely.

He put the picture back, with its face to the wall. 'Now, if you were getting married to some healthy young buck with not much money but a lot of red corpuscles——'

'Like you?' she suggested ironically.

'Like me,' he nodded, unabashed, going through her little wine-cupboard, 'then I'd be right in there at the church door, throwing rice with the best of them. But *Miles*——'

'Yes, Miles!' She walked briskly to the mantelpiece, and turned the picture the right way round again. 'What's so wrong with him? You can't pretend you know the slightest thing about him,' she accused.

'Oh, I know enough about him,' Ry retorted grimly.

'Oh, yes?'

'Oh, yes.' He held up a bottle. 'Shall I open this wine?'

Ginny had the meal ready in a few more minutes, complete with salad and crusty bread, and they sat down to eat. The small oak dining-table just fitted in an alcove that had once been an archway through to the next stable. Everything in the flat was natural, stone walls with big timber beams in the ceiling, clean pale wood everywhere, and clay quarry tiles on the kitchen and bathroom floors.

Ry's presence somehow dwarfed the place. It was so odd to sit down to a meal with him, and watch him wolfing down her bacon and mushrooms. He ate the way he kissed her, with gusto and pleasure. God, how different marriage to Ry would be from marriage to Miles.

Marriage to Ry? The thought almost made her laugh out loud. You'd sooner think of marrying a wolf. And you'd probably see more of the wolf.

'You never got around to telling me how it all started,' said Ry, refilling her glass.

'You mean me and Miles?'

'Yes. I'd like to know.'

'Of course you would,' she said drily, 'so you can find a whole lot more nasty things to say.'

He laid a tanned hand over his heart. 'If I swear I won't say a thing?'

She glanced at him suspiciously, but made a tentative start, all the same. 'I don't really know how it began . . . he's been a friend of the family for so long. It only started *properly* once I joined the bank, of course. That's when we started seeing so much of each other. But ever since my childhood, he's just been so *kind.* So considerate. Miles was always there, you know. Dad had his will with the bank, and Miles was the chief executor. He did so much for us over the years. I remember when Dad died, Miles took care of all the funeral arrangements. He advanced us money until Dad's estate was sorted out. And even when that was all over, he still used to pop in and visit us from time to time, and he always took such an interest in me.'

'I'll bet,' Ry grunted.

'There was nothing like that,' she flashed. 'He's been a tower of strength. He was almost like an uncle to me, until . . .'

'Until you grew out of your rompers,' Ry said meaningfully, glancing at her figure. 'And then, suddenly, he had other ideas.'

'You're so raw!'

'Direct,' he corrected her. 'When did he make his move?'

'Well . . . he started coming more often when I left school. It became a regular visit, every Friday. He started bringing flowers and chocolates for us. At first,' she confessed, 'I thought he was sweet on Mum. She's still lovely, you know.'

'That would seem a rather more suitable combination,' Ry put in drily.

She gave him a sour look. 'Well, as it turned out, he was in love with me, instead.'

'I take it your mother approves of the match?'

'Of course,' she nodded. 'It's a marvellous match for me!'

Ry gave her a twisted smile. 'A marvellous match. He provides the money, you provide the beauty. So he dropped on his knee one day, and fished out that sparkler?'

'No, it was much more gradual than that,' she said. 'Whatever you may think of him, he's a man with very delicate feelings for other people. He had the sense not to rush me or push me. He was just——' Again, she came back to the word that, for her, encapsulated everything that was best about Miles Langton. 'Just so kind. I was no Orphan Annie, being dazzled by wealth, Ry. And he never pushed me, just let me make up my own mind. It wasn't a surprise when he proposed to me.' She gave Ry a challenging look. 'I knew he wanted me, and by then I knew that I wanted him. We're in love with each other. It's as simple as that.' Conscious that her cheeks were mantling with pink, she toyed with her wine-glass, and looked down at her plate. It was odd, but she'd never spoken to anyone like this, not even her mother. 'I *do* want him. He means a lot to me.'

'So does the kind of life he can give you, apparently.'

'You sound like Dodie Witherburn. She doesn't believe I'm sincere either. She never stops reminding me that I'm going to be so much better off once I'm Miles's wife, and that makes me squirm with misery. But Ry, it's true! I *am* going to be better off. I mean, Miles is rich, and I've got nothing. But that's not why I'm marrying him!'

'Isn't it?' Ry asked gently.

'You're horrible! What am I supposed to do? Marry the man I love, but refuse to move into his house, or step on his boat, or take so much as a penny from him . . .?' Her voice tailed off unhappily, and she looked up at Ry with eyes that were starting to glisten with tears. 'You think he's just after me for sex, and I'm just after him for money. How can you think such awful things about me? Don't you know me better?'

'I just want you to answer one thing. Would you still be marrying Miles if he was poor?'

'That's such a naïve question! Miles's money and status are part of him, Ry. He's created his success with his own efforts.'

'And a hefty legacy from Daddy,' murmured Ry. She ignored that comment.

'It wasn't handed to him on a plate. He's worked damned hard to get where he is. And it's part of his achievement. He wouldn't be Miles if he wasn't successful. But to answer your question—yes, I *would* marry him if his success lay in some other field, rather than money.'

Ry studied her. There was so much maturity in his eyes, so much understanding, that she wanted to just throw herself into his arms and cry on his broad shoulder.

'I was surprised to hear you were working at the bank,' he said, easing away from the subject a little. 'You were going to art college to study design, at one time.' He looked up at the pictures on the stone walls, almost all her own work. 'You have talent, lots of it. I love your work. Do you still paint?'

'Hardly at all, now,' she confessed, looking at the portraits and landscapes she'd once done. She gulped down the emotion that had threatened to spill over just now. 'It was all just silly, anyway.'

Ry's mouth, normally so sensuous, tightened into a hard line. 'Silly?'

'Well . . . compared to the work I do at the bank.'

'What decided you on going to the bank instead of art school? Miles again?'

'I decided for myself,' she corrected him. 'But Miles advised me, of course. He pointed out the difficulties.'

Ry shook his head interrogatively. 'Difficulties?'

'Of trying to break into the art world. That it was a long struggle, that it would cost a lot of money, which of course I didn't have.' She toyed with her food. 'That I had to ask myself whether I really had the talent and the perseverance for it. After all, Mum struggled long and hard to put me through the best school she could afford, and it would be horrible to waste all that effort . . . Ry, I'm not going to say another word if you're going to look like that!'

'Have I said a thing? I'm just admiring the work of a master blackmailer. So Miles put you off leaving Grantley and going to college. What then?'

'Well, the bank was an attractive idea. I'd taken a job in a shop for a while, but that had no future. There was a vacancy just at that time, and Miles sort of kept it open for me while I made my mind up. No pressure or anything. I just knew it was there, and eventually I saw the light.' She swallowed some wine, and sighed. 'I'm stopping in a couple of weeks. Wednesday the twenty-third, to be precise. That'll give me a few weeks to enjoy the last of my——' she was about to say "freedom", but changed it at the last moment '—the last of my spinsterhood.'

Ry was neatly mopping up the last of his egg. 'Doesn't Miles like the idea of his wife working?'

'Not in the bank. It wouldn't improve the atmosphere. I might go back again, once we've been married a while. If Miles will let me, that is. Maybe after we've had some childr——' She stopped that sentence before it got any further. 'Funny, I'm going to miss it. I thought it might be dull at first, but it's turned out to be fascinating.'

Miles looked sceptical at the word. 'Handing out money all day in a dump like Grantley?'

'A lot more fascinating than feeding pigs and driving a tractor in a dump like Newton,' she flashed back at him.

'Yes. But as you're so fond of pointing out, I have no ambition. I'm a troublemaker, only fit for feeding pigs and milking cows.' He pointed an aggressive finger. 'Whereas *you*—you are a very special woman. You've got talent, sensitivity, intelligence. It shocks me to hear that you haven't touched a brush since I last saw you.'

'My life has changed.' She looked into the deep blue eyes. 'I've changed. Ry.'

'No.' His voice was quiet, carrying a strange authority. 'You haven't changed that much, Ginny darling. But I think you've taken a wrong turning. I think you're heading down a one-way road that's going to take you to boredom, disillusionment, and despair.'

She stared at him, feeling frozen inside. 'Ry, please stop,' she whispered.

Ry drained his glass, put it down aggressively, and cocked one eyebrow at her. 'I take it Miles hasn't stopped you dancing, as well as everything else?'

'No.' A faint smile broke on her mouth. 'I love dancing.'

'Good.' He rose with that fluid athletic grace, and went over to the stereo set to hunt through her compact disc collection. The recording he picked was smooth, slow jazz, smoky and seductive. He held out his hand to her with a smile. 'Let's shuffle.'

Suddenly, there was nothing Ginny wanted more than to dance with Ry. She rose, kicked off her shoes, and melted into his arms. He held her close, touching her with the whole length of his body, and slid one hand up her back, encouraging her to rest her head on his shoulder.

Through the thin top, she could feel every muscle in his body, warm and hard. Whatever else Ry might be, he was the most beautiful man in her life, physically stronger and surer than anyone she'd ever known. She didn't have to do any dancing at all. Ry was so strong that he made her feel like a drifting leaf in the wind. It was as though he were rocking her in his arms, letting her just relax utterly.

'Do you remember,' he said huskily, 'that night with the Maserati?'

'Will I ever forget it?' She laughed softly against his chest. 'My God, you were so lucky not to go to jail! And if that police sergeant hadn't been a friend of my dad's——' She sighed. 'What prompted you to do such a crazy thing?'

'The same impulse that's prompting you to marry Miles Langton,' he replied calmly. 'I had nothing, not even a mother and father. When I saw that Maserati parked outside the pub, I knew I just had to have it, if only for a night. So I took it.'

'You were only twenty!'

'A very mixed-up twenty.'

'What did it feel like?' she asked curiously.

'Oh, as soon as I got the engine started, I knew this wasn't the way to get what I wanted. It came to me all at once that if I wanted a Maserati, I'd have to earn one honestly.'

'But?'

'But it was far too late by then,' he grinned. 'You know I've never been good at turning back, Ginny. I floored the throttle, and came looking for you.'

The memory was so vivid that she shut her eyes, seeing it all in her mind's eye. Ry arriving in her street in this fabulous, terrifying red sports car, throwing the door open for her. The way she'd got in without a single question, without looking back once.

The way the moon had filled the sky. The way the moonlit roads had unribboned under their wheels as they'd hurtled through the night, down the leafy lanes of their youth . . .

Ginny snuggled against Ry's male strength. 'How did we manage not to hit anything?' she wondered in reminiscent awe.

'My superior driving skill, of course,' he grinned.

Her fingers spread out across his hard shoulders. 'And then we ran out of petrol at the edge of that field . . .'

'No,' he corrected her, 'I only *said* we'd run out of petrol.'

'Why?' she asked, raising her head to look up at him with dreamy eyes.

'Because by then I was bored with the Maserati.' He brushed her temple with his lips, and smiled. 'By then there were more important things on my mind.'

'Ry,' she whispered. His mouth closed on hers, gently and possessively, the way it had done on that moonlight night, when she'd been just sixteen.

For a moment their bodies still swayed in time to the music; and then, as the kiss deepened, they grew still. Ginny's arms stole round his neck, as if of their own accord, reaching up to draw his mouth down harder on hers.

Her lips parted for his tongue, the ecstasy of the kiss

reaching deep into her soul, driving out Miles, Dodie Witherburn, every thought, every responsibility, every doubt. He enveloped her, stronger and sweeter than anything else in her life, and she strained against him, her breasts pressing to the hard wall of his chest.

Their hands were gentle, touching, caressing, getting to know each other's bodies again. Ginny's fingers slid into his thick, crisp hair, ran caressingly down his neck, over his shoulders, on to his arms, up into his sleeves to rest her palms on the hot, naked skin of his back.

It was more than sexuality. They were seeking, exploring, finding something precious and wonderful that had been lost a long, long time ago. Something that had gone out of Ginny's life on the day Ry rode off towards London without a backward look, five years ago. And she was remembering, with a wordless, thoughtless part of her mind, how she'd searched for that something after Ry had left, restlessly and without success.

And then, slowly and hopelessly, she had stopped searching. Since Miles Langton's presence had loomed so large in her life, she had even come to believe that it would never return.

And though her eyes were closed, it was Ry's face that filled her mind, deep blue eyes dancing with challenge and desire. Ry's face, and no other.

The kiss only ended when the record did. In the deep, still silence, they parted slowly, and Ginny passed shaking hands over her face, as though wiping away a dream that she didn't want to remember any more.

'But you never got your Maserati, Ry,' she said in a dull voice. 'You're still milking cows and riding a motorcycle.'

His face changed. 'Does that matter?'

She turned away blindly, and started clearing the things off the table. What had she done? Was she mad? She mustn't let him get so much as a key in her lock, a foot in her doorway——

Ry stopped her, hard fingers biting into her arm. *'Does it matter?'* he repeated harshly.

'It wouldn't matter if you'd won the Pools,' she said, her eyes bright with tears. 'One thing I've learned in my life is that rivers never turn back.' She gestured to the carpet where they'd danced and kissed. 'All that is the past—the dead, forgotten, vanished past. It isn't now. It can't ever be now.'

'Of course not,' he snapped. '*This* is now. You and me, here, talking about your life!'

'If you think you've got any rights over my life, you're wrong.' Ginny pulled her arm out of his grasp and scooped up a pile of plates, oblivious to the knives and forks that clattered to the floor. 'You haven't changed, Ry, but *I* have! Sneer at the new, practical me if you want to. But it *is* me, and I can't change back into an impressionable sixteen-year-old to suit you!'

She hurried to the kitchen, on the verge of tears, and unloaded the dishes into the sink. Knowing that he had followed her, she went on shakily, 'You can't talk me out of marrying Miles with a kiss and a lecture. I love him, even if he *is* rich and middle-aged, and I'm going to marry him!'

'Who says you have to marry anyone?' asked Ry, his voice easy and gentle after the passion of her own statement. 'You're not exactly an old maid yet.'

'I need love,' she said tearfully, turning back to the dishes. 'I need security. I want a family. I'm not going to end up like Jessica Langton, a lonely spinster living on other people's emotions.'

'Let me do that.' He edged her away from the sink, and took over. 'There's something unbearably pathetic about a woman crying over the washing-up.'

Ginny sat back down, and tried to stanch the tears that insisted on flowing, slowly and painfully, down her cheeks. 'God,' she said wearily, 'I should have known better than to let you in. You really know how to upset me!'

'Oh, I try,' he said with a slight smile. He washed up in silence, letting her recover her poise. 'Did I tell you,' he said casually, 'that I've got your pictures all over the walls of my digs in London?'

Ginny looked up, aware of being a lot less than glamorous in her red-eyed, quivery-mouthed state. 'Have you?'

'Mmm.' He rinsed the last plate and put it on the rack. 'When I left, you gave me two of your sketchbooks. Two of the best. They were mostly watercolours of scenes around Grantley, but a couple were portraits. Remember them?'

'Oh . . . vaguely.' She wiped her eyes with a crumpled hanky. 'Are they very awful?'

'They're very good. I've had them all mounted and framed.'

'They must look awfully twee next to the posters of Bruce Springsteen, and Madonna coiled round a motorbike,' she said wryly.

Ry laughed. 'My tastes have refined a little since then. I keep telling you, I'm a reformed man.' He turned to face her. 'As a matter of fact, they look anything but twee. I'd like you to come and see them.'

There was a silence. Ginny gave a little uncertain laugh. 'Is that an invitation?'

'Yes.' He looked into her face, as though to check that she had stopped crying, then kissed her mouth with warm tenderness. 'I'll come for you one of these fine days. It might do you good to see what you're really capable of. Count on it.'

She laughed unsteadily, and reached out to touch the gold ring in his ear. 'This is new.'

'A gift from an admirer,' he grinned. 'Not exactly my style, but maybe I'll grow into it.'

'It makes you look like a pirate.'

'Buy one for Miles,' he suggested, and they both

smiled at the thought of Miles Langton with a gold earring. As the laughter faded from his eyes, Ry said gently, 'I care about you, Ginny. A lot.'

'I almost believe you,' she smiled. Come to think of it, why should she not believe him? Ry did care about her, he showed every evidence of caring. Troublemaker and scapegrace he might be, but he'd always had a very soft spot for her. Maybe he really believed he was doing the right thing in trying to talk her out of marrying Miles.

'The trouble is,' she said gently, 'that you're wrong. Wrong about a lot of things. You assume that I'm marrying Miles for his money and position. That's very far from the truth. My feelings for Miles are genuine. They've got nothing to do with his wealth. Let me ask *you* something, Ry—would *you* have been so concerned if Miles Langton had been poorer?'

'Of course.'

'Really?' Doubt brought a cynical smile to her full mouth.

'What's amusing you?' he asked.

'The thought of you being jealous.'

'Of *Miles*?'

'Of his money. You can be very transparent sometimes, Ry.'

Ry's eyes narrowed. Then he laughed quietly. 'I don't envy Miles his money, I assure you, darling. The only thing that makes me jealous of him is that he has you.' He checked his watch, and sighed. 'Ginny, I'm sorry, but I've got to go.'

She roused herself, hating the thought of being left alone right now. 'Where do you sleep? At Lacon's farm?'

He nodded. 'Harry gives us a room in the attic. It's a bit gruesome—three of us have to share it, and the other two aren't exactly hygienic. But it saves paying rent.'

'Oh, Ry!' Ginny glanced at the sofa in the corner of her little living-room, which had put up guests in the past. 'You could always . . .' she began hesitantly, but Ry shook his head.

'Thanks, but no, thanks,' he smiled. He picked up his jacket, and slung it over his shoulder. 'You'd only regret it tomorrow, and in any case the only way I'd stay the night would be in your bed.' He came over to her, and kissed her hard on the mouth. 'I hope you cry all night,' he whispered, 'you mercenary little bitch! Now come and see me off.'

As he buckled on his helmet in the courtyard, he glanced at her. 'Do you ever see any of the old gang—Sandra Cooper and the rest of them?'

'Hardly ever,' she shrugged. 'Not since——'

'Not since you got engaged to Miles,' he finished, as her voice tailed off. 'Doesn't he get on with them?'

'Not exactly. They're far too young for him.'

'And you're not?' Ry asked with a touch of acid in his deep voice. 'I take it the revulsion was mutual?'

'They never gave him a chance,' Ginny said with a weary expression. 'Just as you're not giving him a chance.'

'Cutting yourself off from everyone of your own age is a rather drastic step,' he said gently. 'You can't have very much in common with the golf club and bowls set. Does Miles ever take you out?'

'Of course,' she said defensively. 'We go to the Country Club twice a week, and we see a lot of his friends.'

'Does he ever take you to the pictures? Dancing?'

'Miles prefers watching videos at home. As for dancing——' she shrugged awkwardly, 'Miles and Jessica are ballroom fans. When I've left the bank I'll take lessons . . .'

He grimaced. 'I can see that your life is going to be one long scream of excitement! I'll be in touch. Thanks for the dinner.'

The roar of the BMW filled the courtyard with energy. With a wave, Ry swung the bike off its stand, and accelerated through the archway into the street beyond.

Ginny stood alone in the darkness, listening to the sound of the engine receding into silence. He hadn't said when she would see him again. *If* she would see him again. The last time he'd left Grantley had been with just such a casual phrase as that. *See you some time, Ginny darling.*

'Ry,' she whispered softly, 'why did you ever leave?'

She turned wearily to go back into her flat, when the light of an open door caught her eye. Margaret Easy was leaning against her doorway, her full figure silhouetted against the light, and Ginny gave an inward groan. The last thing she wanted was to face Margaret.

'Hi,' Margaret said in her husky contralto voice. 'Feel like a cup of coffee and a gossip?'

'I'd love to, Margaret, but I'd better get to bed. I'm so tired,' she excused herself.

'I'll *bet* you are,' said Margaret with unmistakable emphasis. 'That's some man you have there!'

'He's just an old friend,' Ginny said, trying not to sound too stiff. A word or two of idle chatter from Margaret would make untold trouble for her in a town like Grantley. But asking Margaret not to say anything would sound so guilty and stupid. 'We went to school together, that's all.'

'His name's Ryan, isn't it?'

'Ryan Savage. Everyone calls him Ry.'

'Ry—I like that. So it's quite platonic?' Margaret said, sounding almost convincingly surprised. 'Nothing more than friendship?'

'Nothing,' Ginny said firmly.

A sweet smile broke over Margaret's face. 'That's all right, then. Just so's I know. Goodnight, kiddo. Sweet dreams!'

With a wave, she shut the door, and Ginny headed wearily for bed.

CHAPTER FIVE

IT HAD come as a not altogether pleasant surprise to hear that Jessica Langton had already earmarked Ginny's day off for a 'coffee morning' at Greenlawns.

'You don't mind, do you?' Miles had asked brightly at the bank.

'Well . . .' Ginny had struggled between honesty and politeness. Several days ago she'd arranged with Miles to have this Thursday off, planning to spend it with her mother. But Jessica, it seemed, had invited her best friends to come and meet her future sister-in-law before the wedding.

The calm assumption that she would naturally be free to do Jessica Langton's bidding on her day off had galled Ginny.

'. . . it's just that I'd promised Mum I'd go to Westchester with her, to the market. She's arranged to have this Thursday off too, you see.'

'But you're leaving work in a couple of weeks,' Miles had pointed out, leaning back behind his desk, and dipping his head to survey her over the tops of his spectacles. 'You'll have plenty of free time with your mother until the wedding. And Jessica's already invited all her friends. Some of them are coming all the way from London, and they've already made their arrangements. Having to cancel at this stage will make Jessica look foolish.'

'I just wish she'd told me earlier,' Ginny couldn't help complaining.

But her resentment had faded into resignation as Miles had gone on magisterially, 'In a few weeks, Gina, you'll be a Langton, not a Northcliffe any more. You'll be a member of *our* family. And Jessica is a very important member of that family. You'll have to accept the necessity of making the odd sacrifice to her wishes on these occasions.'

'Very well,' she'd said, with as much grace as she could muster, 'I'll tell Mum I can't make it. Please thank Jessica, and tell her I'll be there on Thursday.'

Which was why, on a hot, muggy and rather thundery Thursday morning, Ginny was sitting in the drawing-room at Greenlawns, wearing her best grey suit, with a cup of coffee perched on her knees, being watched by eight pairs of very sharp female eyes.

'They've just gone up and up and *up!* One of the best investments I've ever made. Do you know, I've been able to buy a new car with the dividends alone.'

The speaker was Jean Todd, an expensively-dressed spinster in her early fifties. The subject was a recent issue of shares, of which she'd apparently bought several hundreds. None of these wealthy and mostly single women, Ginny felt, liked her. But Jean Todd liked her the least of all.

She turned to Ginny now, her face an expertly-painted mask of blandness. 'Were you lucky enough to get any of the shares, Gina dear?'

'No,' Ginny said, 'I wasn't.'

'Well, they *were* heavily over-subscribed.' Jean sipped coffee, and smiled sweetly. 'Though I would have thought that Miles, with his connections, would have been able to secure you a few. You did apply, didn't you?'

'I regret that I don't have the money to dabble in the stock market,' Ginny replied with a smile.

'Oh, one doesn't need *money,*' Jean Todd said with a tinkling laugh. 'Not *real* money. A few hundred pounds are all that are necessary, and it's *such* fun.' She tilted her head at Ginny, bird-like. 'I'm sure *everyone's* got that much to spare,' she said, and smiled, obviously waiting for a reply.

Ginny was acutely aware of every eye in the room on her. She knew exactly what Jean Todd wanted to know, what all of them wanted to know. She tried to keep her smile in place.

'I'm sure it's great fun,' she said lightly. 'But I'm afraid that even a few hundred pounds is rather beyond me.'

There was a silence, and then Jean Todd said, 'Well,' in a smooth, satisfied tone, and glanced brightly at the others. They'd found out what Jessica apparently hadn't told them, that she didn't have any money of her own.

'Well, a few hundred pounds won't be beyond you once you're married,' one of the other women, an unlikely redhead, said with a thin smile.

The morning had not been a success. Not in Ginny's terms, anyway. She couldn't help feeling that she'd been very thoroughly weighed in the balance—and found lacking. The implication that she was a gold-digging little nobody had been very explicitly hinted at, and it had brought the colour to her cheeks more than once.

Also, she'd become aware of a feeling she'd often had before—though with Miles, rather than his sister. The feeling that Jessica had done nothing to help or defend her this morning. It was evidently a case of sink or swim for Ginny, and though she was quite capable of rising to the challenge, it wasn't the sort of situation she enjoyed.

Jessica Langton, on the other hand, was clearly enjoying herself. A still-handsome woman in her late forties, with wings of iron-grey in her hair, she was easily the most elegant among her friends. She had her brother's smartness of dress and poise, and her shapely legs, one of which was now crossed over the other, were obviously a source of great pride to her.

Jean Todd reached out to take Ginny's left hand, and studied the sparkling diamond on her engagement finger. Her eyes were malicious. 'I can certainly see one thing—Gina has an eye for the finer things of life. Once she's Mrs Langton of Greenlawns, I'm sure she'll have dull old Miles investing in all *sorts* of things.'

'Will I?' Ginny asked drily, withdrawing her hand, and fiddling with the diamond self-consciously.

'Oh yes, I'm sure you will.' Jean's ice-green eyes crinkled

in another smile. 'You look like the kind of a girl who understands the value of things.'

'I'm not sure that that's a compliment,' Ginny said coolly.

'Aren't you?' Jean just kept smiling and drinking her coffee. Ginny was stinging with resentment. This was Dodie Witherburn all over again, but with teeth. Why didn't Jessica say something? After all, the insult was to *dull old Miles* as much as to Ginny. But Jessica Langton was either sharing in the general fun, or rising nobly above it, because she merely smiled sweetly, and rose from her armchair.

'I'm sure we'd all like some more coffee. I'll ask Mrs Jennings to make some. In the meantime, shall we take a stroll in the garden before it rains? I'm rather proud of the roses this year.'

There was a general exodus towards the garden. The grounds of Greenlawns were beautifully kept, and—as the name of the house suggested—there was a wealth of velvety green lawn in which not a single weed grew. Jessica normally forbade anyone to set so much as a foot on it, but today was obviously an exception. The little party of women, chattering brightly, spread out across the grass in the sultry sunlight. Ginny kept her head down, watching eight pairs of nylon-clad calf muscles tense as high heels sank treacherously into the yielding emerald turf.

One of the kinder women had buttonholed her, and was talking earnestly about the beauties of small-town life, saying how charmed she'd been by Grantley. Listening with a fixed smile and half an ear, Ginny was catching snatches of other conversations going on around her.

The talk was of shares, pension schemes, money, of private schools, of mutual friends she'd never heard of. She felt as out of place among this gathering as an adolescent. What did she have in common with these self-confident, middle-aged and rather malicious women? Almost nothing. She could never call them friends, not even if they'd chosen to accept her. Which they plainly hadn't.

Just within earshot, Jessica was talking to Jean Todd and the dyed redhead about the wedding.

'Yes, the reception's going to be at Greenlawns,' Jessica was saying. 'It seemed silly to go to all the expense of hiring some horrible hotel, when Greenlawns is plainly the grandest place in the town. No,' she added in reply to a question from Jean, 'they're not having a honeymoon after the wedding. Poor Miles couldn't get the time off. This year has been so busy for him.'

'No honeymoon, eh? I imagine *that* didn't go down very well in certain quarters,' the redhead said spitefully.

'Miles is taking her to Wales in the autumn,' Jessica replied easily, 'to make up for it.'

'Still,' said Jean, who was one of those coming to the wedding, 'that saves the silly business of everyone standing around for hours while the bride rushes off to some cubicle and changes into a horrid pink dress which you're supposed to ooh and aah about.'

'Gina's going to change into mufti quite soon after we get back from the church, as a matter of fact,' Jessica smiled. 'Quite a pretty suit in pale cream—my idea. Don't worry, though. You won't have to wait hours. It doesn't take Gina long to put on her clothes.'

'Nor to take them off, I imagine,' Jean said sweetly. 'Poor old Miles!' There was a moment's silence, and then the three women laughed maliciously. Some of the others started edging over, eager to share the joke.

Ginny felt her face flush red-hot. How *dared* they? And how *could* Jessica join in the amusement? Another ripple of female mirth made her stiffen in fury, though her innocently prattling companion didn't seem to notice.

Ginny was really hurt. Yes, these were Jessica Langton's oldest friends. But surely she owed her future sister-in-law some loyalty too?

For the first time, she was feeling something other than respect for Jessica Langton. This had been a horrible morning, and Jessica had done absolutely nothing to make it in the slightest way more bearable for her.

Had Jessica actually enjoyed it?

Ginny shot her a swift glance. Nothing was impossible with Jessica. She was always so poised, so in control. She had always been sweetness itself to Ginny. Yet maybe there were abscesses of jealousy and resentment beneath the calm surface, which had been eased by the spectacle of Ginny being pecked at by her friends . . .

It was an ugly thought, one which Ginny suddenly wished she'd never had.

Mrs Jennings, the housekeeper, appeared at the drawing-room door to announce that coffee was ready, and did Madam want it served outside?

'I think not, Mrs Jennings. It may not rain if we go in, but it will certainly rain if we stay out. Ladies?'

Everyone made their way back towards the house. Ginny gritted her teeth, preparing to face at least another hour and half of scrutiny and malice. She would just sit it out, she vowed, giving no sign that she was in any way hurt by whatever they might say. If this was her ordeal by malice, then she would just have to face it.

Jessica slipped her arm through Ginny's, not seeming to notice Ginny's flushed face and throat. 'You look lovely this morning, dear,' she said, escorting her back inside, apparently quite unaware that she had done anything to give Ginny offence. 'I meant to tell you, I was thinking of going up to Wilson's Nursery this afternoon, to buy some new hydrangeas. The ones near the rockery are looking awfully jaded. Would you like to come with me to help?'

'No, thank you,' Ginny said tightly. She'd done enough for Jessica Langton this morning. 'I'm afraid I've made other arrangements for this afternoon.'

Jessica looked coolly into Ginny's sparkling hazel eyes. 'Have you? Oh, well. It doesn't matter.'

They had to unlink arms to pass through the door back into the drawing-room. Once inside, Ginny moved deliberately away to forestall any further attempt to take her arm.

Jessica's face was smooth and unconcerned, but Jean Todd hadn't missed a second of it.

'Oh, yes,' she trilled to Jessica as Ginny walked away, 'I can see she has a mind of her own. Mark my words, Jessie; once she's Mrs Miles Langton, that girl will be teaching you your place at Greenlawns!'

Jessica was cheerful and bright as she drove Ginny home in her new Mini, a recent birthday present from Miles. It was hard to believe that this Jessica was the same woman who had laughed softly at a nasty joke directed at Ginny two hours ago.

'Sure you won't change your mind about coming to the nursery, darling?' she asked as they arrived at Ginny's flat. 'We could go to the Larches for tea afterwards.'

'I really did promise to go and help my mother,' Ginny excused herself. Even if she hadn't had the excuse, she was feeling distinctly taut after the morning's ordeal, and in no mood for further adventures.

'Well, it's been lovely,' Jessica smiled, leaning across to kiss her cheek. 'A great success.'

She almost sounded as though she meant it, Ginny reflected, trying to give a smile that was sincere. 'It has,' she agreed brightly. 'Thank you, Jessica.'

'My pleasure. Nice to see you enjoying yourself. See you Saturday, as usual?'

'Yes, Saturday, as usual.' Returning her future sister-in-law's kiss, Ginny got out of the Mini and watched it drive away.

Glad to see you enjoying yourself? Was Jessica trying to be funny? Or did she really have no idea that anything unpleasant had been said that morning?

It was still oppressively warm, the threatened thunderstorm rumbling faintly but as yet ineffectually in the distance. Ginny sighed, relaxing her tense shoulders. What a morning! It depressed her unutterably that she found all Miles's and Jessica's friends so uncongenial. Depressed her, and also puzzled her. She usually got on so well with older people. She'd never felt any of the age-gap tensions that some of her friends felt. Why was it that so many of the Langtons' circle treated her with such coolness?

She thought hard about this morning. The nastiness had been there from the start. No, not quite nastiness. More a kind of sharpness in the atmosphere, bracing but not actually unpleasant. But things had steadily worsened from there on. Why? It was almost as though Jessica Langton had been there as a kind of referee. When her friends had seen that she wasn't going to put any brakes on the attack, the pack instinct had taken over.

The same pattern as with Miles and his friends. When they realised that Miles wasn't going to step in and defend Ginny, they felt free to say what they felt like to her.

Letting herself into her flat, she felt a sudden flash of passion. Oh, come on, Ginny, she cursed herself angrily. Don't be so bloody soft. You don't need defending from anyone, let alone a gaggle of schoolmarmish spinsters, do you?

Disgusted with her own depression and weakness, she let out a heartfelt, *'Damn!'*

The deep voice came from behind her.

'Amen to that!'

She turned to face the open door. Ry was standing in the doorway, grinning at her with a sabre-flash of white teeth. 'Someone getting you down lately?' he purred.

'You gave me a fright,' she laughed unsteadily. 'And no one's getting me down. I just tripped on the carpet.'

He leaned against the door-post, tall and incredibly handsome. His cobalt-blue eyes were warm with laughter, as though he was not over-impressed by her story about the carpet. He was wearing tight black jeans, with a beautiful black leather pilot's-style jacket slung over a blackT-shirt. A white silk scarf was carelessly knotted at his muscular brown throat. Miles Langton would have considered the outfit outrageous; to Ginny it was stunning.

For a prodigal, he dressed with considerable style; there was always something about him that stopped her heart, spreading that old ache of desire through her.

'Well?' he smiled. 'Am I allowed in or not?'

'Of course you are,' she sighed, realising she was staring. 'How did you find me?'

'Part planning, part chance,' he said, closing the door behind him. 'I dropped in at the bank to find you, and they told me it was your day off. I came here to look for you, but no luck. Then, just as I was leaving, I saw the fair Jessica drop you off at the archway.' He tilted one dark eyebrow at her. 'Been hobnobbing with big sister-to-be?'

'She had a coffee morning for me at Greenlawns,' said Ginny, careful not to let any of her feelings show. 'I wish you wouldn't go to the bank, Ry.'

'Don't worry,' he said drily. 'I wore these.' He dangled dark glasses in front of her.

'Ah. Those will have helped.' Ginny couldn't help her smile. As if dark glasses could make Ryan Savage in any way inconspicuous!

'Besides,' he went on, 'Brother Miles didn't see me. He was in his little den.'

'Yes, but those girls will talk about you.'

'I love to be talked about. Don't you?' He came to her, and inspected her with smoky-eyed interest. 'God, you look marvellous! That suit is a dream. And that perfume . . .' He leaned forward and brushed her hair with his nose. 'You smell . . . ravishing. When did you get so damned sophisticated?'

'Oh, I'm growing up daily,' she said sweetly. 'I'll be out of my rompers soon.'

But for all her light tone, her nerves were tightening

like guitar-strings as he slid his arms round her waist and pulled her close.

'Ry,' she warned, 'don't——'

'So who was at this coffee morning?' he growled softly.

'No one,' she stammered. 'J-just some of Jessica's girl friends.'

'Sounds like hell.' Gently, sensuously, his mouth closed on hers, pressing her soft lips in a kiss that was half tender, half sexy. 'I've missed you,' he said huskily, his arms strong and possessive around her. 'Have you missed me?'

He didn't have to ask that! Not wanting to give him the satisfaction, though, Ginny shook her head, her face all sweet innocence. 'Naturally not.'

His eyes were the deep blue of an evening sky, smiling and warm. 'Liar!' She could smell the expensive leather of his jacket, the warmth of his skin. He kissed her again, this time with more sex, and less tenderness. How hard his body was, how strong and sure. At the exploratory probe of his tongue, Ginny's already unsteady pulse rocketed, and she quickly pushed away from him.

'No,' she commanded, breathless. 'Not that! Otherwise I'm going to have to ask you to leave—right now!'

'Sorry.' Looking disingenuously apologetic, Ry held up a tanned hand. 'I forgot myself. I was thinking back to five years ago.'

She gave him a dry look. 'Were you?'

'Or maybe it was the perfume. Or that big, luscious mouth.' His voice deepened. 'Or maybe just you. Anyway, I'll behave from now on,' he promised, looking solemn.

Ginny sighed, and slowly her mouth eased into a smile. The last of her tension had suddenly eased out of her. After the catty female company of this morning, Ry's virile male presence was like a tonic.

'I'm going to change out of these clothes,' she said.

'They're far too hot. Could you put the kettle on?'

'Yours to command,' he smiled, giving her a courtly bow.

Feeling ten times better for seeing him, she walked through to her bedroom, kicked off her shoes and pulled off her tights. Formal clothes might suit her, but she never felt comfortable in them. As she checked herself in the mirror, her face was slightly pale, but there were hectic roses in her cheeks, probably the products of Ry's kiss. Good to see him though it was, she wished he wouldn't do that. It disturbed her.

She stepped out of the skirt, took off the jacket, and opened her cupboard to hang the suit up. Right now, she thought, Ry was the perfect antidote to her blues. How lovely it would be to just relax in his company for a while! He would make her smile. He always could. She closed the cupboard, pulled off her blouse, and wearing only a lacy bra and the briefest of bikini pants, paused in front of the mirror to pull the hairpins out of her hair.

What should she wear? Ry always looked so fabulous in denim and cotton. But she hardly had any clothes like that any more. Since Miles had entered her life, her style of dress had changed. Jeans and T-shirts, the sort of clothes that showed off her excellent figure, had gone out. Miles hated to see her 'flaunting her posterior', as he called it. Formal suits and airy dresses had come in. So had weekly visits to the hairdressers, and elaborate styles that emphasised maturity, rather than youth. It was amazing how mature a change of clothes and hairstyle could make you look.

Yet right now she was heartily sick of trying to look mature. She was twenty-one, and for the rest of today she wanted to look it!

The cool air on her naked skin was delicious. Reflected in the mirror, her body was slender, yet sensuous. The darker discs of her nipples, and the delta-shadow of her sex, were just visible through the pretty underwear. The touch of lace added to the innocence of her youthful body, yet somehow made it provocative too. Her legs and arms were slender and beautiful, her waist lithe and taut. Pity, she thought with a wry smile, that she was the kind of girl who looked at her best in bra and pants. And chestnut hair was so ordinary, she mused absently, as she brushed it in the mirror. Everybody had brown hair. Life would be so much more interesting as a platinum blonde, or a raven-haired Latin type . . .

Something made her turn round, suddenly aware that her bedroom door was open, and that her underwear was all but transparent.

Her heart gave a jolt. Ry was standing there, as she'd instinctively known he would be.

She seemed to freeze as she met his dark blue eyes. He had discarded his jacket; the black T-shirt was sleeveless, and his tanned arms were hard with muscle.

He was leaning in the doorway, watching her with an expression that left no doubt as to the kind of emotions he was feeling.

'You're even more beautiful than I remembered,' he said softly, his eyes travelling slowly down her body. 'You've got the sweetest body I've ever seen, Ginny darling.'

'You're supposed to be making coffee,' she said in a choked voice, her skin all gooseflesh at the tone of his voice.

'I got bored waiting for the kettle to boil,' he smiled. His eyes were brooding on her slender thighs, and it was not hard to guess his thoughts. Ginny unfroze at last. Feeling utterly naked, she reached for the first thing that came to hand, a towel. Clutching it to her front, she frowned at him sternly.

'Hasn't anyone told you that it's not polite just to walk into a lady's bedroom?'

'I'm not given to politeness,' he smiled. 'And you're not a lady. You're little Ginny Northcliffe, the only girl

I ever loved.' His eyes met hers, and despite the mocking tone, there was something in them that made her shiver. 'Except that you're big Ginny Northcliffe now. God, but you're beautiful,' he almost whispered. 'Beautiful and desirable and honey-sweet. I wonder whether that pompous stuffed shirt really knows how lucky he is . . .'

'Stop staring at me like that!' she commanded, her cheeks reddening. 'And don't call Miles a stuffed shirt.'

'He's a stuffed something,' Ry retorted, then dismissed the subject of Miles Langton with an impatient shake of his dark head. 'Forget him. You're pale, Ginny. You used to be so brown. Don't you get any sun any more?'

'This is England, remember?' she said, trying to sound flip. 'And I work in a bank, not out in the fields, like you.'

Ry cocked his head on one side. 'Maybe I prefer you like this, though. It makes you look so . . . creamy.'

'I'm not going to stand here and be ogled by you,' she said impatiently.

'Quite right.' His voice was a soft purr. 'Let's make love.'

'What?' she gasped.

Ry was moving forward, his eyes starting to darken with unmistakable eroticism. 'Let's make love. Here and now. We're both aching for it, you as much as me. Why should we keep lying about it?'

'Ry!' she said shakily, backing away. 'Don't'——'

'Don't what?' He was smiling, wicked and intoxicatingly intense, his eyes smoky with passion.

Ginny was still backing away from him, her heart starting to pound, when she bumped into the bed with the backs of her knees, making her sit down with a little gasp. As she looked up at Ry, he crossed his arms and peeled his T-shirt off in one fluid movement. His torso was hard with muscle, his nipples hard with desire against the flawless bronze skin.

He sank down beside her on the bed, his fingers pulling away the flimsy protection of her towel as his mouth sought hers.

Almost panicking in her anxiety to get away, Ginny tried to jump up. But somehow the movement ended abortively, with his arms closing around her, and her towel dropping to the floor.

The contact with his hot, naked skin was shockingly aphrodisiac. She felt the blood surge through her veins as he drew her close, kissing her with a consuming intensity, whispering her name in a rough whisper.

Response was tautening inside her, like a huntsman's bow being drawn to the limit. Though Ry had kissed her with sexual intent before now, there had been nothing as demanding, as hungry as this. There was no way she could resist or evade the fierce passion of his kiss. Her arms stole round his neck, brushing luxuriously against his bare skin, her fingers sliding into the thick, silky curls of his hair.

Every nerve seemed to be alight like a fuse, yet she was also remote from what was happening, far away. There was a rushing in her ears, a floating sensation in her head, as though she'd drunk too much wine, or had lain too long in the sun. Her mouth opened to allow his tongue to enter, exploring, plundering. At her back, she felt Ry's fingers unfasten her bra, and then he was easing her back on to the bed. Like lovers, she thought dreamily. We're lying like real lovers . . .

His fingers trailed down her nakedness, from the hollow of her throat to the top of her panties, then caressed upwards, seeking the swell of her breasts, and the now-aching peaks of her nipples.

As Ry's warm hand cupped her breast, everything changed for Ginny. The floating sweetness gave way with stunning abruptness to a potent reality.

It was not that there was any conscious thought, or any guilt about Miles; rather that, intuitively, she had suddenly understood just how much she wanted Ry. Wanted him, not with a schoolgirl's virginal longing, but with a grown woman's flaring hunger. Need was like a bush-fire out of control; not a pleasurable, controllable response to being kissed and caressed by an attractive man, but rather an elemental force which frightened as much as it aroused.

Lying near-naked in Ry's arms, it was as though she'd suddenly realised she was standing on a cliff-edge, about to fall into a bottomless void.

The prospect was delicious, yet profoundly terrifying. Making love to Ry could be no stolen pleasure; it would change everything, for ever. There could be no marriage to Miles if this went any further. She would be Ry's, unable to contemplate a life without him. She had to stop him now, or there would be no return!

Ginny felt the muscles of her body tense in a spasm of reaction, and then Ry released her with a startled noise of pain.

She stared at him dazedly, watching him touch the blood on his lip with his fingertips, then shake his head in wonder.

'You little vixen,' he said softly.

Shakily, she leaned forward. There was a neat, semi-circular cut on his lower lip, oozing bright blood. She realised with disbelief that she'd bitten his lip hard enough to break the skin.

'Oh, Ry!' she said with a tragic expression. 'God, I didn't mean to——'

But he was grinning at her. 'Talk about boundless passion! Where did you learn a trick like that?'

'I don't know—my muscles just tensed——'

'You're telling me!' He was reaching for her again, undeterred by his bleeding lip, and it suddenly occurred to Ginny that this was her only chance to get away before the onslaught started again.

Like a salmon escaping a net, she swung herself frantically off the bed and made for a cupboard. A white cotton shirt was to hand, and she pulled it unceremoniously over her tousled head, covering her naked, tingling breasts as quickly as she could, then started pulling on the first pair of slacks she found.

Ry was lying on the bed, watching her with an amused, rueful smile. 'The one that got away,' he said gently.

'I'm so sorry about your lip,' she panted, zipping up her slacks. 'I don't know what got into me——'

'Forget it. It was worth it,' he said, watching her dress. 'I hate to repeat myself, darling, but you're so beautiful . . .'

'You're not so bad yourself,' she said, tucking her shirt into her slacks, and feeling ten times less vulnerable. She turned to him, putting on her sternest face. 'But that is taboo, Ry. I mean it.' She tried to disguise the uneven note in her voice. 'It isn't allowed any more. It's forbidden.'

His stomach muscles came into hard relief as he laughed quietly. 'It was marvellous, though. Worth any number of cut lips! Tell me something . . . do Miles Langton's kisses do that to you, Ginny?'

Ginny looked down at him in silence, as though Miles's name were a word in a foreign language. It was impossible to imagine Miles lying like this, half-naked on her bed, looking up at her with that slow smile.

Impossible to imagine Miles kissing her or touching her like that, with such confidence.

Ry was different. Ry was so intensely male, his sexuality emphasised by the black hair which spread across his chest, and crept down his flat belly towards his loins. Ginny looked away, the blood rushing to her face.

'The kettle will be boiling itself to a frazzle,' she said clumsily.

'I know how it feels,' he said, rising to his feet with liquid ease. Ginny inspected his lip with remorse.

'That looks so sore. I can't believe I did it. Wait, I'll get a plaster for it.'

'No,' he smiled. 'I'll just have to answer a lot of

embarrassing questions from the lads at Lacon's farm about how I got it!' He slipped an arm round her waist, and as she tensed, shook his dark head. 'Don't worry, this is friendly. Let's go and get that coffee.'

They sat in the kitchen, talking relaxedly, just feeling the tension in both start winding down. Ginny wondered whether Ry knew, as they sat here so calmly, drinking coffee and discussing old times, that her body was still yearning for him, her fingers trembling round the cup, eager with readiness? Those moments in the bedroom had been so intense—almost frighteningly so. There had been a wild, pagan quality about the kiss that had shown her things about herself she barely knew existed.

But she didn't want to think about that, and her thoughts shied away from the subject. It was better to just pretend that things like that didn't happen, and to treat Ry like the old friend he was.

There had always been intimacy between them, an intuitive understanding of each other's thoughts, and Ginny sank blissfully into the warmth of Ry's companionship.

If only poor Miles knew how much she missed the company of young people! It didn't seem to occur to him that she might need the friendship of people her own age, that she might want to talk about the things young people talked about.

Miles could offer a security that Ry couldn't. But oh, how she had to pay for that security!

It felt so good to have Ry here, filling the little flat with his male presence, his beautiful, half-naked body so alive and healthy. He radiated a quality that Miles would never have. Ry was utterly physical, a man who enjoyed life with great zest. When he kissed her, it was as though nothing in the world was more important, or more precious to him. Yet that was exactly the way he rode his motorbike, or enjoyed a meal—or did anything he really enjoyed. It was just Ry. You had to remember that it wasn't you, that you weren't special in any way.

He would make you feel wonderful, like the only woman in the universe.

And five minutes after leaving you, he would have forgotten you utterly!

Out of his arms, she could see everything in perspective again, her mind unclouded by passion. How many girls, she wondered, had mistaken that intense sexuality of Ry's for deep emotion? It was an easy mistake to make. Ry was the most completely desirable man she had ever known. But she must never lose sight of the fundamental point, the thing that Ry could never give her—complete safety.

With Ry, she was always aware that the dark period of her life, the period of loneliness and insecurity, was waiting in the wings, threatening her happiness. With Miles she never had that feeling. Miles did not possess a tenth of Ry's vitality, his energy; yet Miles spread an aura of calm and security around her that was almost tangible. His authority, his wealth, even the fact that he was so much older than she was, all helped to give her a feeling that she was protected, cherished, safe from all harm. And that quality, she had to remember, was worth all Ry Savage's sexiness . . .

The afternoon melted away in intimacy and relaxation. There was so much to say, so much to fill in, that she was shocked to suddenly notice the time on the kitchen clock.

'Damn!' she exclaimed. 'I should have been at my mother's three hours ago!'

Ry smiled. 'Don't worry, I'll take you.'

'On the bike? No, thanks! I don't want the whole of Grantley talking.'

'The bike's still at the garage. I've got a car.'

'That's different,' she smiled. 'Though I find it hard to reconcile the idea of you sitting in a car. Isn't it a bit too civilised for your tastes?'

'Wait till you see the car.' He reached for his T-shirt

and pulled it on again. Ginny watched the ripple of iron-hard muscles, the flash of black hair at his armpits, and felt her loins start to ache. 'Ready?' he enquired, getting to his feet.

Ginny sighed, and nodded. 'I'll just get a bag.'

Five minutes later Ry was walking her down the street, one arm possessively through hers. He was wearing his jacket now, but that didn't make him any the less striking, and Ginny was acutely aware of feminine eyes swivelling to follow them. There just wasn't any way of being inconspicuous with Ryan Savage. Yet she couldn't help the squiggle of pride at having him on her arm. At least she knew she was the envy of every female under ninety in the place!

But when they reached the car, Ginny's eyes widened in shock.

'Oh no!' she exclaimed in horror. 'Ry—you haven't!'

'Haven't what?' he asked innocently.

Ginny stared at the blood-red Ferrari gleaming in the dull sunlight. It was a convertible, its top down to expose luxurious cream leather seats and an opulent walnut dashboard.

'You haven't—*borrowed* it, have you?'

Ry laughed with genuine pleasure. 'No,' he smiled, opening the door for her, 'not in the sense you mean. I've grown out of that by now. But I am driving it on someone else's behalf.'

Ginny eyed him suspiciously, not moving to get in. 'Whose behalf?' she demanded.

He shook his head in mock-disappointment at her suspicions. 'It belongs to Keith Lacon, old Harry Lacon's son. He asked me to bring it to the garage here for new front tyres.' As she hesitated, he pointed patiently to the front offside tyre, which *was* plainly new, still wearing yellow chalk-marks on its otherwise immaculate sides. 'Look there. Believe me now?'

'Sort of . . .' Finally, though still not altogether

convinced, Ginny allowed herself to be ushered into the seat. She sank into it deliciously, and ran her fingertips along the gleaming dashboard. 'I've been in a Maserati,' she smiled, as Ry got in beside her, 'but never a Ferrari.'

Ry shrugged. 'They're strictly for rich maniacs, like Keith Lacon. But I rather enjoy running errands in it.' He slipped his dark glasses on, looking so perfectly the part of a rock-star millionaire that Ginny giggled.

'You're going to break a lot of hearts, going around like this.'

He twisted the ignition key, and the engine exploded into life, a deeper, harsher note than the motorbike, but equally exciting. Ry guided the car out of its parking place and accelerated briskly up the street.

'This car suits you,' she told him, reaching out to touch his long, thick hair with her fingers. 'If you got a proper job, you could save up and buy one.'

He smiled at her rather wryly. 'I'd sooner have an hour with you, on that bed, than any number of Ferraris.'

'You'd be better off with the Ferrari,' she said, her turn to be wry. 'It's nice of you to pretend, but I know exactly how ordinary I am.'

'Meaning?' he asked, glancing across at her.

'If I'd let you make love to me, at the flat, you'd have lost interest in me completely by now.' She smiled. 'To you, I'm the one that got away, nothing more.'

Ry didn't answer, and she lay back in her seat to enjoy the drive.

But you mean so much more to me, darling Ry, she thought sadly. She'd enjoyed those hours with Ry with an intensity she'd almost forgotten could exist. He'd made her feel young and happy again, and she hadn't felt either for a long, long time.

But driving with him in this fabulous car was somehow sad. It made her think of what might have been, of the life Ry could have had if he had just realised a tenth of his potential. Was he going to spend the rest of his life as a drifter, running other people's errands in other people's sports cars?

It brought home even further the difference between Ry and Miles Langton—Miles, who had acheived so much, who owned houses and cars and boats, Miles who could offer her a security Ry would never understand.

If only there were someone who could lift Ry out of the pointless life he had chosen, and help him to reach the goals she knew he was capable of reaching . . .

She'd once thought that she might be that person. But it had never happened. Ry had turned his back on Grantley, and on her, and had set off on a trail of his own. And there was nothing that she or anyone could do for him now.

I'm supposed to be getting married to another man in a few weeks' time, she thought sadly. *But I don't know how I can bear to lose you.*

CHAPTER SIX

HER MOTHER didn't get off work till five-thirty, so Jessica Langton went with Ginny for the first fitting of her wedding dress on Tuesday evening.

Miles had made it clear that he was paying for the dress, yet another example of his kindness. It was fortunate, as Jessica remarked, that Mrs Beeston was such a good dressmaker, because a London wedding dress with that much silk would have cost a fortune. But Mrs Beeston had been making wedding dresses for two generations of Grantley brides, and the design she had worked out with Ginny was going to look a dream.

'Although *personally*,' Ginny's future sister-in-law said critically, 'I might have chosen artificial flowers instead of real ones.' She was sitting in a chair in Mrs Beeston's parlour, her slender ankles crossed. Any coolness between her and Ginny since the morning of the coffee party had evaporated by now, and she was displaying nothing but warmth towards Ginny. 'For one thing, there's much more scope for disaster with real flowers. And for another, you'll always have the artificial ones as a keepsake. Real flowers will just wither.'

'I've got a thing about artificial flowers,' Ginny confessed. She was too ashamed to tell Jessica that it was due to a childhood memory of the silk flowers in her father's coffin. The undertakers had placed a wreath of satin roses on her father's chest, and the sadness and incomprehension of that day had left her with a lasting distaste for artificial blooms of any kind. That was why she'd decided on real roses, cream and white, for her bouquet and headdress.

'Real flowers,' Mrs Beeston said through a mouthful

of pins, 'is always nice for a summer bride.'

In fact, they were using paper ones while the dress was being made, to get the final effect. The 'dress' was just a collection of roughly-cut pieces of white silk and lace at present, but the seamstress was pinning and marking with the confidence of long practice. She rose from her kneeling position, puffing a little with the effort, and surveyed the result with a bright eye.

'Take a look, dearie,' she invited.

Ginny shuffled cautiously over to the full-length cheval mirror, and stared at her own image. The dress was still only a sketch, but the impact was almost shocking.

A bride, in a traditional long white gown, was staring back at her from the glass, wearing her face, her wide eyes.

'Oh!' she sighed. 'It's *lovely,* Mrs Beeston!'

The two older women flanked her to look into the mirror, Jessica tall and slim, Mrs Beeston short and fat.

'Yes,' Jessica said slowly, 'that really *is* lovely, Mrs Beeston.'

Ginny was just staring at herself. There was an odd feeling in her heart. Nothing had brought the reality of her impending marriage home to her like this moment. Wearing the holy white, the transparent veil, she felt a heavy solemnity descend on her. She was getting married. *Married.* She would be leaving her home, her name, her maidenhood and her freedom behind her, for ever.

The memory of herself in Ry's arms on Thursday afternoon came unbidden to her mind, sudden as a clap of thunder, and she looked down, her cheeks flooding with guilty colour.

'There,' Mrs Beeston said in delight, 'bless me if the child isn't blushing like a rose!'

'This isn't the time for modesty, Gina.' Jessica patted her shoulder. 'Don't be shy. Look at yourself.'

Ginny just shook her head. How they mistook her

emotion! God, the intensity of that kiss, the feel of his hand on her breast! And the long, treacherously delicious hours of companionship afterwards . . . Tears were horribly close.

Oh, Ginny, she thought miserably, which is the real you? This white-veiled bride, or the near-naked girl who'd kissed her childhood sweetheart on Thursday afternoon? She didn't deserve to put this dress on! Bitterly ashamed, and unable to even look at herself any more, she turned away from the mirror.

'Take it off,' she pleaded unhappily.

'Oh, don't be such a goose!' laughed Jessica. She turned Ginny back to the mirror with strong hands. 'And don't you dare cry. You look ravishing. Miles is going to be bowled over. What do you think of yourself?'

Forced to face the image, Ginny met her own eyes. The look of unhappiness on her face went oddly with the bridal white. With an effort, she cleared it away, pulling herself up straighter. Mrs Beeston, smiling broadly, passed her the bouquet they'd mocked up, and Ginny held it across her left breast, the way she would do when she walked up the aisle of St Cuthbert's Church.

'Pretty as a picture,' Mrs Beeston murmured softly.

Ginny tossed her head back a little, and met her own eyes again. Yes, she was beautiful. And she would make a beautiful bride. Mrs Miles Langton. The bells would clatter joyously in the morning sunlight for her as she emerged from the cool, dim church, with her husband on her arm. And her past would be behind her, for good.

Thinking of that, something happened inside Ginny, a moment of conscious decision.

She knew what she wanted. Not the dangerous, impermanent excitement that Ry could offer, but the deep, lasting value of a stable marriage with Miles.

She thought again of that burning, stolen kiss, but this time she didn't blush. That must never happen again, never, never. She couldn't afford to let Ry Savage near her. She would avoid even the sight of him from now until her wedding day. Then she would be safe.

She'd seldom spent such miserable days as these past few. Ry's visit had left her with a continuous sick pain, with broken sleep and guilty dreams. She'd felt unable to look Miles in the face, and she'd had to excuse her downcast eyes and drooping head with a silly lie about a summer cold coming on.

No more.

She had to face herself now, and take command of her wandering emotions. She had to see things clearly, clear as this bridal white.

Yes, Ry was attractive. She'd always been half in love with him as a girl, and he still had the ability to exercise a strong seductive power over her. He would always mean a great deal to her. But she had to face the fact that Ry would never be her husband.

And yes, she *had* experienced doubts about her marriage to Miles. Doubts were natural. It was healthy, even essential, to question a decision as important as this one. Maybe Ry had even done some good, by helping her know her own mind.

Because she had to be certain where her real desires lay, and work out what was the best thing for her own life. No one else could do that for her. Especially not someone as irresponsible and prejudiced as Ryan Savage. And at this moment, she knew that marriage to Miles Langton was what she wanted.

It was not the ardent passion of a movie heroine, no. It certainly wasn't the feelings she had for Ryan Savage. But there were many kinds of love, and the love she felt for Miles was based on trust, respect, affection, and security. She had no doubts about his feelings for her, and she knew that he could make her happy. He could offer her a home unthreatened by change or instability, a life that was secure, a marriage that was insured against loneliness and indigence.

She'd been hurt by all those insinuations that she was only marrying Miles for money and status. But those things entered into it too, and Ginny suddenly felt that she would never be ashamed of them again. She'd said it all to Ry. Miles' wealth and position came from his competence. Therefore she must accept his standing in Grantley as a part of him, an essential factor in her future husband's make-up.

Damn Ry for the thorn of doubt he'd pushed so firmly into her heart! It had taken her all this time to pull it out, and she knew the bruise would last for ages longer. What right did he have to cause her so much misery? As if he had any authority over her life! As if he'd achieved anything in his own life! What was Ry? If the truth were to be known, he was probably a minor criminal. A failure, who came to the country in the summer months to labour on a farm and dream about his lost innocence. He was a beautiful animal, intensely sexual; but he would never make any woman a decent husband. To compare him to Miles was so absurd that it was laughable.

'There,' Jessica Langton said approvingly, 'that's better.'

Ginny had unconsciously straightened up, and the expression on her face had changed to one of firm-lipped resolution. She met her future sister-in-law's eyes in the mirror, and smiled.

'Do you like it, Jessica?'

'Of course. Mrs Beeston was absolutely right about the silk.'

A soft, musical voice came from the doorway. 'Can I come in?'

'Mum!' Ginny swung round in pleasure to face her mother. 'What do you think?'

Prudence Northcliffe came into the room, smiling greetings at Jessica and Mrs Beeston. She was still wearing the checked smock she wore to work, at the garden centre just outside the village, but she looked fresh and young.

She gave Ginny a quick, tender look. 'It's going to be lovely, sweetheart. You look so happy.' She turned Ginny round to look at the back view. 'Beautiful, Mrs Beeston. It reminds me of my own wedding dress.'

'Not far off,' Mrs Beeston nodded complacently. 'You two's got the same figure. Neat.'

'I'm just a bit concerned about Ginny's choice of real flowers,' Jessica put in, and explained her objections.

Prudence Northcliffe listened carefully. Jessica was older than she was, and an altogether different type of personality, and the relationship between them was one of cautious mutual respect, rather than affection.

'Ginny hates artificial flowers,' she said at last. 'It goes back to something that happened when she was a little girl. It upset her terribly, and she's detested them ever since.'

'Yes,' Jessica shrugged, 'but she's a grown woman now. Artificial flowers are so much more suitable——'

'I think real flowers would suit Ginny rather better,' Ginny's mother said, smiling to take any sting out of the contradiction. 'It's really her choice, isn't it?'

Jessica looked as though she were going to argue further, but then gave a graceful shrug. 'Far be it from me . . .'

The rest of the fitting was conducted without controversy, and when there was no more to be done, they agreed to have a cup of tea in the cake-shop round the corner together.

'Now,' Mrs Beeston said, fiddling with the headdress, 'before I start unpinning it all, is there anything you want different? Any changes you want done?'

'No,' Ginny said firmly. She gave the bride in the mirror a last, confident look. 'It's just perfect as it is, Mrs Beeston. I don't want any changes at all.'

* * *

As usual on a Wednesday night, Ginny was at the Country Club with Miles and his sister for the weekly smörgasbörd dinner. Although a courteous invitation always stood for Ginny's mother to accompany them on such occasions, she almost always refused. If that was an indication that she'd ever received a disappointment at Miles's hands, then it was the only one she ever gave, and her ostensible reason was a dislike of rich food.

The food was indeed both rich and delicious, ranging from smoked oysters and mussels to cold meats and exotic salads, and was laid out on long buffet tables. As usual on these occasions, the dining-room was crowded.

Fighting her way back to Miles and Jessica through the bustling throng, Ginny reflected that being wealthy and privileged didn't make people any the less ruthless when it came to self-service food. Trying to edge past corseted hips and energetic elbows, she had a childhood memory of once getting caught up in a herd of cows on their way to milking, and having to be rescued, shrieking, from the unheeding mêlée.

'Phew!' she panted, finally getting back to their table with her plate more or less intact, 'some of those *people*——!'

'You're too little,' Jessica smiled, watching Ginny rub an ankle with a rueful expression. 'Miles, you really ought to get Gina's food for her.'

'Not everybody recognises her yet. They'll pay more attention once we're married,' Miles promised. 'Catch anyone stepping on the chairman's wife's foot *then*!'

'I look forward to being treated with suitable reverence,' Ginny said wryly. 'I'm delicate.'

Miles smiled. 'So how's The Dress getting along?'

'You're not supposed to know a thing about it,' Jessica said firmly. 'But I think I can tell you that it isn't actually hideous.'

'It's beautiful,' said Ginny, starting on her salad. 'Mrs Beeston is really very good.'

'She's got a good model.' Miles glanced at Ginny's dress, a ravishingly pretty pink frock that breathed of summer. 'You wear everything well,' he said approvingly. 'When you've got more money to spend on your wardrobe, Gina, there won't be a woman in Grantley to touch you.'

'Except Jessica,' Ginny put in.

'Oh, I'm well aware that I don't count for anything,' sighed Jessica, pretending to be offended. 'I'll just go out to pasture when you two are married.'

'Nonsense,' Miles said briskly. 'You'll still be the mistress in my house.'

'How can you say such a thing?' Jessica retorted. 'Gina will be the mistress, of course.'

'Gina will be my *wife*,' Miles said in a firm tone. 'You're the mistress of Greenlawns, and you always will be.' He gave a Ginny a glance. 'You wouldn't want it any other way, would you, Gina?'

'I'd hate to think I was upsetting your household in any way,' Ginny said cautiously.

'As a matter of fact, I'll be jolly glad to have someone else wash Miles's socks and underwear,' said Jessica. 'There's nothing particularly alluring about the job.'

'You know very well that the housekeeper takes care of all that,' said Miles, reddening slightly. The two women smiled at each other. It took only the vaguest reference to underwear to embarrass Miles. 'This is a silly conversation, in any case,' he went on forcefully. 'There's no question of Gina displacing your position in the household, Jessica. You've been running things extremely successfully for twenty years, ever since Mother died, and I see no reason why you should stop now.'

'Perhaps we can rule by committee,' Jessica suggested cheerfully. 'You can't expect Gina to have no say at all in how things are run.'

'Not that, either. It will simply confuse the servants to have two mistresses to answer to.'

'What do you intend her to do all day, then?' Jessica wanted to know.

'There'll be plenty for Gina to do.' Miles cleared his throat. 'Especially when we have—er—a family of our own.' Miles touched Gina's hand, the most he ever did in public, and gave her a warm look. 'Gina can have anything she wants, of course. She has only to ask. But while you are alive, Jessie, Greenlawns will be run *your* way.'

Jessica shrugged slightly, smiled, and kept silent. Embarrassed by the whole conversation, Ginny concentrated on her food. This wasn't the first time Miles had brought up the subject, but he'd never been quite so positive about it before. Miles could be very tactless for such a suave man . . .

Not being mistress in her own house was a rather disquieting thought. On the other hand, Miles was right; Jessica *had* been running Greenlawns ever since their parents had died, and it seemed absurd for Miles's elder sister to have to defer to a woman nearly thirty years younger than herself.

Furthermore, Ginny knew it would be a long time before she could run a big household with Jessica's flair and efficiency. She'd watched Jessica organising servants, deciding menus, planning the garden, doing the hundred and one things that went into daily life at Greenlawns, and she'd been rather overawed. Jessica Langton's schoolmarm manner worked very well with servants and tradespeople, and she seemed able to exercise an effortless authority that Ginny felt she herself would never possess.

What the hell, anyway? Ginny gave a mental sigh. As Jessica herself had just said, it wasn't really an enviable post. It might be fun to be a lady of leisure for a few years . . .

When the conversation re-started, it was on a completely fresh topic, and Ginny was rather relieved.

At around eight-thirty that evening, though, when they'd dropped Jessica off at Greenlawns, and were alone together on the way back to Ginny's flat, Miles brought the subject up again.

'I hope you weren't offended by what I said earlier this evening,' he began. 'But I wanted to get things clear between the three of us.'

'No, I wasn't offended at all,' Ginny said.

Miles parked the Jaguar near the archway, and turned to her. 'It's not that I don't have any confidence in you,' he said seriously. 'But you *are* very young, and my sister does have—will *always* have—a very special place in our household.'

'Of course,' Ginny nodded. 'I get on very well with Jessica.' Which was just as well, she thought wryly, or the situation might have been a damned sight more difficult than it was.

'I know you do. And I'm very pleased.' He took his pipe out of its little pouch, and started filling it slowly. 'I've never told you this, but my father's will gave the house and nearly all the money to me. Jessica has a substantial annuity, and some jewels of my mother's, and that's all. Everyone expected, of course, that she would marry. But she didn't, and my duty is clearly to take care of my sister as long as she lives. I take that duty very seriously.' He looked into her eyes. 'Jessica means a great deal to me. Our getting married is not going to change that.'

'Oh, Miles,' Gilly said gently, 'you don't have to explain.'

'Hear me out,' he insisted. 'I regard Greenlawns as Jessica's house, as much as it's mine. It will always be her home. I think she would be bitterly hurt to find herself supplanted and cast aside by a young wife. That would be intolerable.'

'I have no intention of supplanting or casting aside anyone,' Ginny said coolly. 'If you want Jessica to continue running Greenlawns, I have no objections at all. She does the job far better than I ever could, anyway.'

'Exactly.' Miles fiddled with his pipe. 'It's always been my wish that in time you'd come to see Jessica as rather more than a sister-in-law. It would please me greatly if I thought you saw her as a——'

For an awkward moment Ginny thought he was going to say *mother*. But instead he said, '—a real sister. An elder sister whom you could look up to and learn from.'

'I can only repeat that I get on very well with your sister,' Ginny replied.

What more could she say? It wasn't altogether pleasant to be told, seven weeks before her wedding, that she was to have no status in the household. On the other hand, status in Miles's houshold was not something she could demand. The situation was unusual, in that Miles and Jessica were so close, and so much older than she was. She would have to make compromises, that was all.

She hoped that she and Jessica would be friends, given Miles' insistence about the household, and she would try very hard to make things work. But she was marrying Miles, not Jessica, and it was her relationship with her husband, rather than his sister, that was going to be important. She hoped that Miles understood that!

'I'll do my best,' she said with a sigh. 'You know I will.'

Miles appeared satisfied at last. 'That's all right, then,' he smiled. 'You'd better get your beauty sleep.' He touched her arm. 'Not having second thoughts about our marriage, are you?'

'Of course not,' she said, slightly startled. 'Why do you ask?'

He watched her with keen eyes. 'The past couple of weeks you've been . . . what's the word? Distracted. Broody. Looking as though you were feeling very uncertain inside.'

'It was just that summer cold,' Ginny lied with a smile. 'It never materialised, after all. I've had all my second thoughts, Miles. My mind's as made up as yours is.'

'I'm very glad to hear it.' He reached for her, his goodnight kiss warmer than usual, his expressions of affection tender.

She watched the Jaguar's tail-lights recede in the dark street, five minutes later. Though it was a warm summer's night, she was cold, starting to shiver.

It was an internal coldness. Ginny recognised it, with something like dismay, as dread; the same dread she had felt as a child when her family had tried to break the news of her father's death to her.

But what did she dread? Marriage to Miles? She'd felt so positive about her marriage in Mrs Beeston's front parlour. Now, depression had unaccountably settled over her again. What was wrong with her? She'd known she would be taking second place to Jessica Langton; she'd resigned herself to that a long time ago. Why should that cast new shadows over her mind?

This to-ing and fro-ing of her emotions was infinitely wearying. She was starting to be incapable of holding her mood for more than a few hours, it seemed.

It was *absurd* to go up and down like a yo-yo from day to day! Either she was going to marry Miles or she wasn't. Either she knew her own mind or she didn't.

The trouble was that when she was confident, she was *very* confident. And when she was uncertain, she was miserable . . .

She stopped short in the archway, her heart skipping a beat.

Ry's motorbike was parked in the courtyard again. And again, Margaret Easy's door was ajar, the yellow light spilling into the courtyard.

He'd come to see her again. But she couldn't face him tonight. Not the way she felt right now, so vulnerable and depressed. Trying to sneak into her own flat unnoticed was silly. In a moment, her mind was made up. She turned, and walked swiftly down the street towards the bus station, where she could see one of the red local buses parked at the stop. She'd go to her mother's cottage, and spend the night with her. There were fresh clothes there, and she'd be able to get the bus straight back into work tomorrow morning.

Ginny was so intent on getting away before anyone saw her that it wasn't until the bus was pulling out of the stop that it occurred to her that she was effectively leaving Ry in Margaret Easy's clutches.

For a moment, a pain lanced through her heart like a shooting star.

Then she shook her head angrily. What a stupid, irrelevant thought! She had no right to be jealous over Ry and Margaret. They were nothing to her.

The key to regaining her lost composure was to cauterise this irrational feeling that anything special still existed between herself and Ry. It was with Ry that all her doubts and fears had originated. Well, leave them with him! If Ry chose to spend the night in Margaret's arms, that was hardly her business. In fact, it would be a good thing if he did. It would remind her exactly what sort of man Ry Savage was.

Was Ry the sort of man to sleep around indiscriminately? Of course he was! Remember Tina Harpur, the barmaid at the Crown, the prettiest woman in Grantley? Ry had been just a kid when she'd taken him to bed. Ry had lost his virginity at sixteen, and had never looked back. And given Margaret Easy's considerable charms and welcoming nature——

Ginny felt the pain lance through her heart again, keener now, aware that with every moment the bus was taking her further away from Ry.

Should she have stayed, gone to face him, if only to stop him from spending the night with Margaret?

Jealousy. Such a strange, shameful emotion, so painful, so hard to deal with. But that was what she felt right now, burning jealousy of Margaret Easy, who tonight would lie in Ryan Savage's arms.

She felt her fingernails biting into her own palms, her teeth clenching involuntarily.

'You're the only girl I've ever really wanted to bed.'

'That's only because you've already bedded all the rest.'

'Maybe.'

Yet she and Ry had never made love. Her own virginity was testimony to the fact that, while he might have desired her, he had never tried to take her to bed. Last Thursday had been the only time he'd really wanted her. And that had only been because the opportunity had presented herself, and he'd walked into her bedroom while she'd been almost naked.

Kissing her, holding her, playing the part of the devoted lover—that was all just part of his anti-Miles campaign. Maybe it was even just his version of a compliment. But didn't she want him? Wasn't she, even now, on the verge of bitter tears because she wanted to be in Margaret's place tonight?

Some engagement. What sort of woman, practically on her wedding eve, would have feelings like this? First, uncertainty about her marriage partner. Then, sexual longings for another man!

She twisted in her seat, hating herself for the line her thoughts were taking, hating herself for wanting Ry so much, so very much . . .

She didn't need all this doubt and confusion. She'd been so happy until he'd reappeared on the scene. If she could have submitted to an operation, there and then, that would have removed every memory of Ry from her heart, she would have done it.

But the feelings ran deep. She'd always wanted Ry. That night in the stolen Maserati had been the first time they'd kissed. For her, the first time she had ever kissed.

She'd melted in his strong arms, exactly the way she'd melted the other day, feeling her soul yearning towards his, her newly mature woman's body filled with a wild, disturbing ache.

She could remember in vivid detail the caress of Ry's tongue, the intense, heedless passion that their embrace had released. That stolen summer's night, a vast and unexplored universe had unfolded all around her . . .

If the police hadn't arrived, blue lights flashing, they might have made love there and then, on the leather seats. The thought of it now, even after all these years, was flooding her with that aching desire, her secret body responding to the memories as though they'd been physical caresses.

Ginny closed her eyes. There had been other times after that, other kisses, other embraces between her and Ry. But though she herself might have been ready, more than ready, to make love, it had always been Ry who had held back.

It had been a crowning irony that on the one occasion when Ry had really wanted to make love to her, last week, it had been *she* who had held back!

That was partly why there was so much tension in their relationship. It was the tension of strong physical passions held in check, of fulfilment denied. Of yearning that never found release.

Her forehead creased in concentration. Why? Why did Ry always hold back? Wasn't she that desirable, after all? Did busty, husky-voiced Margaret have qualities that she lacked, qualities that a man like Ry might prefer in his sexual partners?

She could see them in her mind's eye, Ry's beautiful, muscular body locked with Margaret's——

With a little gasp of pain, she sat up in the seat, and opened dull eyes. This kind of brooding wasn't getting her anywhere. She had done the right thing tonight.

The right thing.

She was Miles Langton's fiancée, soon to be his wife. Five weeks from now, in the big double bed in Greenlawns, it would be Miles who took her virginity. On that night, his lovemaking would drive every thought of Ry Savage out of her heart. And then she would be his woman, to the end of her days.

The years would come, and the years would go, and Ry would just be a memory. A harmless memory, without danger, without pain.

She had to cling to that thought. After all, wouldn't it be wonderful to have a life free of yearning for Ry, free of the ache of missing him?

Wasn't that one of the reasons she'd agreed to marry Miles in the first place? Yes. Yes, her marriage to Miles had grown directly out of her experience with Ry . . .

Ginny stared out of the window into the night, lost in her thoughts, watched by her own shadowy reflection.

Later, asleep in the little spare bedroom at her mother's cottage, she had the dream again. She'd had it before, or a dream very similar to it, but never so frighteningly intense as this.

She was in a huge, echoing Underground station, somewhere in Central London. She didn't know where she was going, but she knew with overwhelming horror that she was always heading in the wrong direction.

She fought her way through faceless crowds, down packed corridors that were a jumble of meaningless sound. Sometimes she was on towering escalators, that were always going the wrong way, carrying her towards a destination she feared.

Until finally, exhausted by her long struggle, she reached the platform. The train was there, and she threw herself through the doors, just as they were closing. They crashed behind her, shutting her in the compartment. It was full of strangers, whose eyes surveyed her without friendship, without mercy.

But when the train jolted into movement, it, too, was going the wrong way. Despair and frustration made her cry out, and she pushed vainly against the doors.

They did not open. Instead, the train picked up speed, rushing into the tunnel. And just before she entered the long, pitch-black corridor, Ginny saw Ry, standing on the platform, waving to her and calling.

Desperately, she tried to catch his words, to signal back, but he was gone. And there was nothing but darkness all around her.

CHAPTER SEVEN

'HAVE a good time the other night?'

Ginny's head snapped up, and she found herself staring into Ryan Savage's incredibly blue eyes.

She straightened on her stool, her mouth suddenly dry. 'Shouldn't you be feeding pigs?' she enquired coolly, not at all pleased to see him in the bank this Friday morning.

'It's my morning off,' he said succinctly. His eyes were still on hers. There was something subtly different about him this morning, maybe the fact that he'd shaved, and was wearing a cool-looking red check shirt and smart jeans. He looked almost smart.

He also looked grim, and rather formidable. 'Where the hell were you that evening?' he asked, leaning on the counter.

'That's none of your business,' she said crisply. 'I take it you spent a pleasant evening of your own—with Margaret?'

There was a blue glitter of anger in those deep eyes. 'Then you knew I was waiting for you. You deliberately stood me up.'

'I don't believe we had an appointment,' she retorted. 'Is there anything I can do for you, Mr Savage?'

'Yes,' he said. 'I'd like to deposit this.' He heaved the black leather bag on to the counter. Suspiciously, Ginny opened the till window. The bag was immensely heavy, and she could hardly move it across to her side.

When she opened it, she saw the reason why. It was filled with money-bags, the buff canvas kind. About three hundred pounds' worth of copper and small silver.

'I see,' she said joylessly. 'Have you been robbing telephone boxes?'

'Parking meters. Actually, I decided to break into my piggy-bank,' said Ry. 'That bag represents years of savings.'

Ginny gave him a tight-lipped stare. She'd made up her mind that the next time she faced Ry, it would be with resolution and defensiveness, and this little joke was helping her do just that! A small queue had started forming behind Ry already.

'Excuse me,' she said briefly, and made for Miles' office. 'Can you put someone on the other till for a bit?' she asked. 'A customer's arrived with half a ton of small change.'

Miles nodded, and came out with her. As his eyes met Ry's, though, she felt him stiffen like a gun-dog at her side. With a sinking feeling, she knew he'd recognised Ry.

'Mr Savage, isn't it?' he said in a voice that was equally stiff.

'Good morning, Mr Langton,' Ry nodded easily. His ultramarine eyes, though, were cold in his tanned face. 'Any problem?'

'None,' Miles said shortly. He gestured at the bag of coins. 'Would you care to come back when this has all been counted?'

'I'd rather wait right here,' Ry said smoothly. 'I'd hate to think of any of my pennies going missing.'

'As you please.' Miles walked away to ask one of the others to take up the third till. His face was expressionless, but Ginny knew him well enough to tell that he was angry. She felt tension tighten every nerve in her body. Damn Ry for coming in here today! She'd have given a lot for Ry and Miles not to have met like this . . .

Ginny got the weighing machine, and sat back at her till. Whatever had brought Ry into the bank this morning, she was determined that this was not going to take long!

She dropped the first bag on the scales, and checked the reading. According to the value printed on it, it was wrong.

'This one's short,' she said irritably. Ry shrugged slightly. She checked another one. 'And *this* one's got too much in!' she exclaimed. With growing anger, she weighed several more. They were all wrong.

Ry was watching her, laughter somewhere deep in those vivid blue eyes.

'This isn't very funny,' Ginny said tightly, and opened one of the bags. There was no way of telling what all the copper coins really came to. She would have to sort the whole lot by hand, a job that she really hated. As a way of monopolising her attention for half an hour, this was an effective but very dirty ploy. Unreasoning resentment made her almost hate him at that moment. Damn him, *damn* him and practical jokes!

'You don't look very welcoming,' he grinned, as though her evident displeasure had assuaged his own anger.

Ginny's reply was terse. 'I would have thought you'd have worked it out by now, Ry. I don't want to see you any more.'

'Is that so?' He sounded unperturbed. 'That's a very sudden decision. A week or so ago, you were in a rather more intimate mood!'

Ginny's eyes dropped to his lip, where a neat scar indicated the damage her teeth had inflicted. She felt her face and throat flush hotly, and she started sorting the coins in silence, packing them into bags of the correct measure.

'So you saw the bike,' Ry went on, 'and turned tail. Didn't you have any qualms about leaving me in the clutches of the fair Margaret Easy?'

'You seem to get on with her well enough,' Ginny said shortly. But she was remembering with sharp clarity the utterly miserable night she had spent, wondering about Ry and Margaret. No, not just wondering. Imagining, visualising, *knowing*. And then that ghastly dream on the Underground, Ry's figure disappearing in the blackness . . .

Shuddering slightly at the memory, she flicked some more coins into a bag, then couldn't help asking in a strained voice, 'How—how long did you wait that night?'

'None of your business,' Ry replied. Ginny looked up fiercely for a moment, her eyes darkening. 'I was well entertained,' he smiled, 'put it that way.' If he noticed the flinch of pain that crossed her face before she dropped her gaze again, he gave no sign. 'And where were you all night? Dancing the light fandango with Brother Miles at the Country Club?'

'None of *your* business,' Ginny retorted. That flippant reply had cut like a whiplash, and the pain had sealed her curiosity once and for all!

'Quite right,' Ry smiled, 'it isn't.' His eyes were serious, though. 'Something's happened to change you, Ginny. What?'

'Nothing's happened,' she gritted. 'I just think the time for games is over.'

'Has Miles been getting his hooks into you? Is that it?'

'No, that isn't it. But Miles knows we used to go out,' she said tersely. 'This is a stupid and cruel thing to do.'

'Ginny, I want you to come to London with me.' It was said decisively, as though he had no doubts about her acceptance. 'Tomorrow. For the *whole* day. And after that, if you don't want me to ever bother you again, I swear I won't. That's a promise.'

She felt anger prickle under her fine skin. 'I don't care what it is, I'm not going anywhere with you!'

'Then you're going to have to put up with a lot more

bother from me,' he said meaningfully. 'I'm a very persistent man.'

She was close to really hating him. 'If you were a gentleman——'

'But I'm not a gentleman.' His eyes were intent on her hands, mindlessly doing their job. 'So you'll have to think of some other kind of appeal.'

'That won't be hard to find,' she said in a hard voice.

'Meaning?'

'Meaning that if I tell Miles how you've been bothering me, he'll call the police, and have you marched out of the village!'

The second the words were out of her lips, she regretted them bitterly. Ry's deep eyes just lifted to her face with lazy contempt, and Ginny shook her head quickly, shame dispelling the anger at him. 'No, I didn't mean that—I'm sorry. But I meant everything else I said. I'm not going anywhere with you. The game seems to amuse you, but I'm not playing with you any more. I'm engaged. You can't just breeze back into town and pick up the ends of a flirtation you dropped a year and a half ago!'

The expression in Ry's eyes changed. 'It never was a flirtation,' he said quietly. 'It was always more than that, Ginny.'

'Not on my side,' she said hotly.

'It was on mine. And I can't sit idly by while you drift into a marriage with that——' his gaze flicked across to the door of Miles's office, '—that heartless tailor's dummy.'

'Ry!'

'Not to mention dear Jessica.' Ry's smile was hardly pleasant. 'Now there's a strong character. She's been keeping her brother in order for the past thirty years. How does she feel about handing the job over to a younger woman?'

She didn't answer, just kept her mouth in a tight, hurt line. Ry went on drily, 'You do realise that you won't count for a thing in that house? Between the two of them, you'll be nothing more than a songbird in a cage. Pretty, ornamental, and fundamentally unimportant.'

She kept a seething silence, hating the accuracy with which he could strike at her weakest places.

Ry nodded slightly. 'I see you've already started realising that. Do you really imagine you can live the way they plan you to?'

Her fingers felt numb and clumsy as she closed the next bag. Why did Ry's words have such power to shock and depress her? She didn't need any extra pressure, not right now. She was under enough strain as it was. 'If you really do care about me,' she said in a low voice, 'then for God's sake stop doing this to me! You have no right to come in here, putting your oar in——'

'Don't be silly,' he retorted. 'I have a perfect right. You mean the world to me.' He was more deeply tanned than ever, but he wasn't wearing the earring this morning. Ginny glanced at the tiny hole in his earlobe. Odd how something that would have made another man look effeminate merely made him look all the sexier.

Confident in his own stunning beauty, he gave her a slow smile. 'Have you ever considered how easy it would be for me to *really* put my oar in? A few words with dear Miles about the good times you and I shared? What if I tell him we're still lovers?'

Ginny stared at him in disbelief. 'I would never have believed this of you.'

'Oh, I'm quite ruthless where my friends are concerned, Ginny.' He looked totally unabashed by her dark, accusing stare. 'It must have been a long time since you got out of Grantley, even for one miserable Saturday.' He leaned forward persuasively. 'Isn't it worth it? A day in London for the privilege of never seeing my smiling face again?'

She met Ry's bright eyes for a moment, thinking of those dreadful Saturday afternoons at the Witherburns' bungalow. 'Why do you want me to come to London so badly?'

'Many reasons. To show you your own paintings. To get you away from here. To spend some time with someone I care very deeply about.'

The last words were spoken very gently. Her hands moved mechanically through the task she was doing. Ginny took the next bag in her hands, feeling its heavy weight almost unconsciously, and stared at him. Even if she'd wanted to, there was no way she could get away. 'How can I?' she asked with a sense of hopelessness. 'I can't just disappear for a whole day without telling Miles——'

'Tell him the truth. Surely he trusts you to spend a day with an old friend?'

She thought of the way Miles would see it, the way he had stiffened as he recognised Ry. 'No! He'd be furious . . .'

'Then tell him a lie,' Ry said brusquely. 'You'll be doing plenty of that in a few months' time. You might as well start getting some practice.'

Ginny glanced up at him. At that moment, with some kind of telepathic intuition, Miles himself came back to the till. He was still wearing that expressionless face, his dark eyes unreadable behind the lenses of his spectacles, but Ginny could feel his anger clearly.

He cast an eye over the bags of small change. 'Everything all right?' he asked Ginny. Ry's eyes didn't miss the slight but proprietorial touch on her arm that accompanied the question.

'Fine,' she nodded briskly, concentrating on her counting.

'Good.' Miles turned to Ry with a passable imitation of a smile. 'May I ask what brings you such a long way from home, Mr Savage?'

'You seem to forget,' said Ry, meeting his gaze calmly, 'Grantley is my home.'

'Oh? I had the impression that your home was in

London these days. You've been living there for some years, have you not?'

'Yes.'

'In which case,' Miles went on, with an elaborate politeness that grated on Ginny's nerves, 'Grantley is no longer your home, is it? Just as this is not your branch. It puzzles me that you should come so far out of your way to bring this money here.'

'It puzzles you?' drawled Ry. 'You sound as though I owe you an explanation.'

Miles glanced sharply at Ginny, then back at Ry. 'Perhaps you do,' he said meaningfully.

'What an odd attitude!' Ry's smile was mocking. 'But then this *is* Grantley. I'd forgotten what busybodies small branch managers can be.'

Ginny felt herself go cold at the insult. Miles' face turned a slow brick red. 'I have a perfect right to make an enquiry about anything that happens in my bank,' he said stiffly.

'The bank does not belong to you,' Ry said coolly. 'Not even this branch. Don't exceed your jurisdiction, Mr Langton.'

Miles gestured at the heap of money. 'This is a deliberate waste of my staff's time,' he said, growing hotter as Ry grew cooler. 'It hasn't even been counted properly before it was brought here!'

'That's what tellers are for, aren't they?' Ry asked easily. 'This bank wouldn't last very long if it regarded taking money as a waste of its staff's time.'

Miles made an effort to control his temper. 'Perhaps I expressed myself badly,' he said coldly. 'My puzzlement concerns why you chose this particular teller, not just why you chose this particular branch.'

'Oh, I see.' Ry laughed softly. 'It's about Ginny, is it? You shouldn't let her work on the till if you don't want her to speak to other men.'

'As it happens, Gina is leaving the bank in a week's

time,' grated Miles. 'And after that, I see no reason why she and you should ever have reason to encounter one another again.'

'You talk in circles,' Ry said contemptuously. 'If you object to my speaking to Ginny, why not just come out and say so?'

'If you compel me to.' Miles's moustache was bristling. 'I don't interfere with Gina's friendships in any way. She is free to see whom she chooses. But I do *not* regard you as a suitable companion for my fiancée.'

'In other words,' drawled Ry, 'you *are* interfering with Gina's friendships?'

Ginny, feeling dizzy with tension, glanced around. She was certain that everyone in the branch could hear this bitter little quarrel developing, and she wasn't reassured by the fact that no one seemed to be looking their way. 'Miles,' she said quietly, 'I think it would be better——'

'I intend to have my say,' Miles said icily, cutting her off. 'You may think I'm a fool, Savage, but I'm not. Don't think I haven't realised that you've been pestering my fiancée in the most public fashion. You've gone to her flat uninvited. You've driven round with her, flaunting yourself, in an open-topped car. You even took her on the back of your motorcycle through the middle of the town, as though she were some common——' Miles spluttered back the words. 'I've let it go on this far, because it's not my style to use the heavy hand. But I know what your little game is, and it's now past a joke!'

Ginny sat very still. So Miles knew about Ry's visits! A heavy depression washed over her. Of course he knew. He knew everything that happened in Grantley.

'You amaze me,' said Ry, his face still relaxed and smiling. 'You're even pettier and smaller-minded than I remembered. If Ginny wants to see me, what on earth makes you think you've got the right to stop her?'

'I've got the right to protect my future wife from any

kind of nuisance,' Miles said with unmistakable menace. 'In any way I choose.'

'That's terrifying,' said Ry, his smile widening. 'But are you sure Ginny regards me as a nuisance? Why don't we ask her?'

In the taut silence that followed, Ginny was aware that she was shaking. Both men were watching her, and she grimaced tiredly.

'This is hardly the time and place for a quarrel,' she said in a low, unsteady voice. She knew what she had to say, and now was the moment to say it. 'But if you both insist on being so childish——' She took a breath, trying to steady her tone. 'I told you not to try and see me again, Ry. I'd prefer it if you respected my wishes. It would be kinder to me, and easier for everyone.'

When she at last lifted her haunted eyes, he was looking at her with something like pity on his handsome face. But there was no anger, no other emotion in his gaze.

Miles spoken again, curtly. 'That concludes the conversation, Savage. You can take this as an official warning-off. I hope I won't have to say any of this again. Because if I do, you'll have cause to regret it.' He tapped Ginny briskly on the arm. 'Close down the till when you've finished with this gentleman. I'd like to see you in my office as soon as you've done so.'

He turned on his heel and walked off.

Ryan's gentle laugh shocked her.

'I'm glad you think it's funny!' she said fiercely. 'Why couldn't you damned well *listen*?'

Thank goodness, she'd reached the last bag. She tied it with a jerk, and wrote the final figure down. She filled out the deposit slip, stamped it, and passed it across the till to Ry. 'Two hundred and seventy-five pounds. Satisfied with your morning's work?'

Ry pocketed the slip without looking at it. 'What a stuffed shirt that man is,' he smiled. 'Can you really feel any respect for him?'

'The answer is yes. And I'm rapidly losing all respect I ever had for *you*!'

'He's been spying on you,' Ry said gently. 'You do realise that?'

'No.' Ginny rejected the accusation with a brisk shake of the head. 'It's your fault. Nothing happens in Grantley without a lot of gossip. Maybe that's what you wanted, after all . . . A blind man couldn't help noticing the way you've been chasing me.' She was on the verge of tears, and fighting hard to keep them from showing. She prepared to close down the till. 'Please go,' she said. 'You've done enough damage for one——'

'Wait.' The command stopped her, and she met Ry's fierce gaze with eyes that were starting to blur.

'What?'

'My offer still stands, Ginny. If you come with me to London tomorrow, you'll just have to say the word, and I'll disappear out of your life. For good.'

He was so obstinate . . . Ginny could only shake her head, wondering whether Ry Savage would ever learn. She would have given a great deal for this morning never to have taken place. She was going to have to face Miles now, and explain just why she hadn't told him about her meetings with Ryan Savage, and she really didn't relish the prospect——

'I'll be at your flat early tomorrow,' he said quietly. 'If you want to take up my offer, I'll be ready. You'll have all night to make your mind up.'

Without another word, he turned and walked out of the bank. She watched his tall, wide-shouldered figure, the virile way he moved, and felt like something caught in a vice. Then she pulled the shutter down, and went back to face Miles.

He was sitting behind his desk as she came in. She shut the door behind her, and met his cold eyes.

'Miles,' she began, 'I'm sorry about what happened

just now——'

'Don't be,' he said in a clipped voice. 'I expect crudeness from that type of man. He's little better than a thug.'

Ginny winced. 'I didn't know that you were aware he was seeing me,' she went on. 'I expect you're wondering why I never told you about it.'

Miles smiled icily. 'I think I'm entitled to some kind of explanation, yes. Don't you?'

'The reason is quite simple. I just didn't want you to be upset, Miles.'

'Upset?' he repeated ironically. 'Why should I be upset at something so irrelevant?' He paused frigidly. 'Unless you have something further to tell me?'

'Oh, Miles!' She sat down heavily opposite him. 'Nothing *happened* between us, if that's what you want to know. It was all quite innocent.'

'You're lying,' he said with a coldness that made her eyes widen in shock.

'What?'

'You're lying to me. It has *not* been all quite innocent. That much is obvious, by that man's attitude, his *insolence*——' Miles almost spat the word out. 'He is not innocent, and neither are you, Gina. Given his attitude just now, I can well guess the purpose of his visits. He's trying to talk you out of marrying me, just like all the rest of your so-called friends. Can you deny that?'

Ginny met his eyes. She owed him the truth. 'No,' she said quietly, 'I can't deny that.' Miles face darkened with anger, but she went on, 'The important thing is whether he convinced me or not. And I think I've just demonstrated that he hasn't.'

Miles drummed his fingers on the desk. 'I expect he wants to marry you himself, is that it?'

'Ry? Marry me?' Despite the tension, she couldn't help laughing out loud.

'What's so amusing about that?' Miles demanded

angrily.

'You don't understand . . . He hasn't a bean in the world. He works his summers as a casual labourer on local farms, and I'd rather not know what he does in London during the winter! Ry isn't the marrying kind, Miles. And even if he were the marrying kind, he's not in any position to support a family.'

Miles stiffened, as though she'd said something insulting. 'Is that the only reason you prefer me to him? Because I'm richer?'

'Of course not,' she sighed. 'It isn't a question of me preferring anyone. I'm engaged to you, and Ry means nothing to me.'

'He once meant rather more than nothing to you,' Miles said sharply.

'That was a long time ago.' She looked down, smoothing the skirt over her thighs. 'Before I met you.'

'Exactly.' His eyes were cold and hard through the lenses of his glasses. 'You were much more than *just friends,* weren't you?'

She avoided his eyes. 'Not in the way you mean.'

'Oh? Ginny, I want the truth. The *whole* truth. Have you been sleeping with that man?'

Disbelief made her stare at him for a moment. Then, her face colouring hotly, she rose to her feet.

'I've got work to do, Miles.'

'Wait, damn you!' He reached across the desk, his fingers closing round her arm with surprising strength. 'This isn't some kind of asinine, juvenile game,' he grated furiously. 'You were that man's lover, weren't you? If not now, then before?'

'No,' she said tightly. 'It's none of your business, but I was never Ry's lover. Not before, and certainly not now!'

'Do you expect me to believe that? When you let him kiss and touch you in public?'

'Yes,' she said bitterly, wrenching her arm free, 'I

expect you to believe me, Miles. I'm telling you the truth. You heard what I said to him this afternoon. What more do you want? A sworn statement?'

The telephone on Miles's desk shrilled in the frozen silence, and Miles scooped it up impatiently.

'Yes? Yes, very well. In a moment.' He gave Ginny a grimace as he replaced the receiver. 'The bank isn't the place for this discussion. We'll talk about it tonight, before we go to the Country Club.'

'All right,' she nodded, still stiff with anger.

'And now, I've got a client to see.' Miles rose, straightening his lapels, consciously easing the anger out of his face. Somehow he looked smaller now that the anger had left him. His voice became calm and well-modulated again, as though nothing had happened between them. 'Will you do those standing orders, please? They're on Vera Davidson's desk.'

Ginny nodded. Feeling numb, she got up and walked out of his office.

'What upsets me,' said Miles, staring out across the courtyard, 'is that you concealed it from me all this time.'

Ginny bit her lip. 'It seemed so unimportant at first . . .'

'Unimportant?'

'Well, yes.' The late afternoon sunlight was warm and golden across the stonework. Parked in their usual place opposite her archway, Ginny had been trying to explain about Ry. She was struggling hard not to tell Miles lies; yet how could she admit that she had had Ry in her flat, had let him kiss her, without giving him a ghastly misinterpretation of what had really happened?

Miles was now evidently in control of his anger, but she knew he was still upset, and she was treading warily.

'You know that Ry and I were once . . .' she hesitated, 'once friends. He feels he has the right to give me advice, no matter how misguided it might be.'

'Misguided is right.' Miles looked into her eyes. 'I think I ought to tell you something, Ginny. I rang his London branch a week or two ago, after . . . after I got word that he was pestering you. I had a little chat to the sub-manager about Mr Ryan Savage. He gave me some very interesting information about our friend. It turns out that your suspicions were well founded. The man is almost certainly a crook.'

'Why do you say that?' Ginny asked, a steel hand clenching round her heart.

'He has no fixed job. No employers. That's odd, for a start, wouldn't you say?' Miles's smile contained no humour. 'One is inclined to wonder what he lives on. Yet live he does. He deposits peculiar amounts at irregular intervals, invariably in cash. And he goes through the money like lightning. He runs up big overdrafts, then suddenly clears them off. Always with cash—with used notes. Now what does that suggest to you?' Apparently unaware that Ginny's face had turned grey with unhappiness, Miles went on, 'He pays no taxes and keeps no books. It's the characteristic pattern of the petty criminal, Ginny. I've been a banker long enough to recognise the signs a mile off.' He took a sheaf of paper out of the walnut-veneered glove compartment. 'He has a bank-backed credit card. Would you like to see the kind of thing your dear friend Ry spends his money on?'

'No,' she said in a low voice, feeling sick. 'This isn't right, Miles.'

'I'll give you a précis, if you're so squeamish. Pleasure, alcohol and women. About the only other things he lays out his cash on are clothes and his motorcycle.' He tossed the papers contemptuously back into the glove compartment. 'Most of it goes on drinks. There are endless receipts from nightclubs, casinos and hotels.' Miles grimaced. 'And worse places. He clearly isn't above paying for his sex. Or maybe he just prefers the company of prostitutes.'

Ginny turned away, her eyes bright with tears. What else had she expected? She'd guessed what sort of life Ry was leading in London, so this oughtn't to come as a shock to her.

But the pain inside was overwhelming. Somehow, somewhere, she'd always had the hope that Ry would triumph over his critics in the end, that his wildness would subside. He had great talents, she knew, and she'd always hoped that he would fulfil his potential one day, and not stay a troublemaker all his life. That hope had just taken a nose-dive into the mud.

She had a sudden vision of Ry standing at the river bank, in the golden sun, with little Lucy asleep in his arms. How could someone so beautiful, so gifted, have gone so wrong?

'Damn,' Miles said softly, watching her face. 'Do you really care about him that much?'

'He was a friend,' she said with a catch in her voice. 'Oh, Miles, I feel so sorry for him. He never had a chance! He didn't have any parents, and he was always in trouble of one kind or another . . . yet he's capable of achieving so much, if he only had someone to guide him.'

'And you think you could be that someone?' Miles demanded bitterly. 'Is that it?'

'He doesn't care about me.' She fought back tears. 'Not in that sense. I don't have any illusions about that. But *someone* could help him, maybe someone like you. Someone older, wiser——'

'You must be joking,' sneered Miles. 'I wouldn't touch him with a ten-foot barge-pole!'

Ginny shook her chestnut head unhappily. 'You only see the worst in him, like everybody else. But I know there's good in Ry, I *know* there is. If only someone would help for once, instead of condemning him.' The words burst out of her. 'What's going to become of him, Miles?'

Miles snorted. 'That's not our concern or our business—thank God.' He clenched his teeth. 'There's something about that man that makes my blood almost boil. Maybe it's because I know how you used to feel about him. Maybe because he's so different from me in every way.' His expression was bitter. 'He's the kind of man most women dream about, isn't he? Handsome, virile, immoral. I've seen the way the girls in the bank look at him. As though they were dying of thirst, and he was a pitcher of cool water . . .'

'Miles, don't,' she pleaded. She'd got herself under control now, and the tears had remained unshed. 'Whatever I once felt for Ryan Savage is now in the past. For good.'

'I believe you.' He smiled tiredly. 'I just want him to stay away from you, and from Grantley, from now on. That kind of man doesn't belong in a decent, quiet village like this. He exerts an influence that is . . . evil.'

She couldn't help denying the exaggeration. 'Oh, no. He's just a troublemaker. Ry may be wild and irresponsible, but there's not an evil bone in his whole body. He may be a petty criminal, as you say, but I can't believe he's anything worse.'

'I take him more seriously than you do.' He took a deep breath, and tried to smile. 'I was on the edge of cancelling our engagement this morning, do you know that?'

'Miles!' she cried, her heart twisting inside her.

'I was so depressed,' he confessed, squeezing his temples. 'The longer you kept silent about Savage's visits, the more convinced I was that something was going on . . .'

'And you knew all along.' She glanced at him with shadowed eyes. 'How?'

'Oh . . . people told me,' he said evasively.

'Which people?'

'People close to you.'

'There isn't anyone close to me who . . .' Suddenly, she guessed. 'You mean Margaret Easy?'

Miles hesitated, then nodded. 'Yes.'

'I didn't know you even knew her,' Ginny said, thinking of Margaret's sly smile and veiled questions. There was an uncomfortable feeling between her shoulder-blades at the thought of Margaret watching her all this time, reporting on what she did to Miles. 'And I didn't know Margaret was that type,' she added, in a drier voice.

'Margaret Easy has an account at the bank. A personal loan, as it happens.' Miles's expression was almost smug. 'As I'm sure you know, she lost her job some time ago. We've made things easy for her. What with one thing and another, she owes the bank a favour, as you might say. When you moved into the flat next door to hers, I asked her if she would . . . keep an eye on you.'

'Be your spy?' Ginny asked, with some bitterness.

'Just watch over you,' said Miles. 'Make sure you were all right. Don't look so shocked,' he added, catching her expression. 'I didn't particularly like doing it, but as it's turned out, it was a wise precaution. It's saved us from a potentially very ugly situation.'

Ginny turned away, feeling something like disgust, but Miles reached for her hand, lacing his fingers through hers. 'Gina, be an adult. This isn't a game, you know.'

'I know,' she said in a low voice.

'I want you to tell me if he ever comes near you again. Immediately. Don't try and deal with him on your own. He's far more dangerous than you, in your innocence, can possibly imagine.' Miles's expression changed subtly. 'Leave him to *me.* I know the right people to deal with Mr Savage's problem. People who speak the sort of language he understands.'

'What do you mean?' she asked, wide-eyed with alarm.

'I mean that if he ever comes near you again, I'll make sure he regrets it for the rest of his days.' He smiled at her appalled expression. 'Don't look so frightened. It's a hard world, and sometimes one has to be hard to face up to it.'

She felt unhappiness well up in her, like a vessel about to overflow. A nightmare seemed to be closing in around her. 'Miles, for God's sake don't do anything stupid. Ry's not that serious a threat, and violence——'

'Who mentioned violence?' he said soothingly. 'I have influence, that's all I mean. All sorts of influence. If Mr Savage hasn't learned his lesson yet, we'll have to find some better way of teaching him it.' His eyes narrowed. 'Unless, after all I've told you about him this afternoon, you persist in feeling squeamish about him?'

'I don't want to see him hurt in any way,' she said tensely. 'Whatever he is now, he was once my friend!'

'Oh, I'll remember that,' Miles assured her with an icy smile. 'If I ever have to deal with him again, I'll certainly remember that.'

CHAPTER EIGHT

GINNY had hardly slept, unable to rest peacefully in her single bed, which either seemed too hot, or too cold, or too small, or too large. The things Miles had said to her about Ryan Savage kept echoing in her mind, producing images that were ugly and sad. Eventually, in the early hours, she had dozed off in exhaustion; but her sleep was thronged with nightmares, just like the night she had left Ry at Margaret's.

The dreams evolved towards a moment of sheer horror. She was standing on a road, at night. The flashing blue lights of ambulances and police cars fitfully illuminated the scene of a disastrous accident. A motorcycle had collided with a big, expensive car. In cold terror, she was trying to make sense of the mangled wreckage.

Whose was the car? Whose was the motorbike? Whose body was being lifted out of the twisted steel and rubber?

She moved forward, her skin icy with fear. The face of the dead man rolled sideways, streaked with blood. It was Ry. And behind him, Miles sat behind the wheel of the car, laughing.

Ginny awoke, choking on her own cry of anguish, and found herself sitting up in bed, covered in a cold sweat.

It was well after dawn, and her room was filled with early morning sunlight, softly filtered through the curtains. Still living the horror of her nightmare, her heart thudding against her ribs, she climbed out of bed and threw open the curtains. How horrible dreams could be, how real. All one's fears and anxieties surfaced in them, taking monstrous shapes. Of course Miles could never hurt Ry like that.

She'd just been shocked by the ugliness of his threats

last night. She'd brooded on them too much, taking them far more literally than they were intended.

Ginny looked up at the duck's-egg-blue sky over the rooftops, and breathed deeply to calm her fluttering nerves.

It was just another normal Saturday, with a normal weekend coming up. Her wedding was one week closer. This afternoon would be spent with Dodie and Edward Witherburn, and this evening with Jessica at Greenlawns. Tomorrow she would spend the day with her mother, and in the evening go to the Country Club with Miles and Jessica.

The nerves of her stomach tightened in sudden rejection. For a moment, a deep revulsion at the prospect of this weekend, of hundreds more weekends like it, rose up in her like nausea. Could she really face the years and years of such days that stretched ahead of her?

Ginny closed her eyes on the morning sky, feeling herself sway slightly, and clung to the window-frame with cold fingers. For God's sake, she wasn't going to faint, was she? The rushing in her ears subsided slowly as she fought the feeling down.

She hadn't eaten last night. Nor yesterday lunchtime. That was it. She was half starved. And still disturbed after her dream. Nothing more.

After a few minutes she opened her eyes again. The nausea was still there, in her throat, but more under control now. She swallowed it down, like bitter medicine, and consciously straightened her back.

How stupid to be so weak and irresolute!

It was just another normal, enjoyable weekend, with everything under control, and everything going smoothly. After a shower and breakfast, she would feel her old self again.

Ry was coming here this morning, fully intending to take her to London with him.

Her heart jumped painfully at the thought of meeting

those vivid blue eyes again. She turned away from the window, and hauled off her nightie, preparing for a shower. Well, it was time for an urgent conversation with Ry. This time he had to understand that this game of his couldn't go on. It had to end, now.

And not just for her sake, either. After the conversation she'd had with Miles last night, she'd be insane to show any weakness now. Miles had meant those threats; and though she didn't believe he was capable of violence—she thought of her dream again, and shuddered—he was certainly capable of hurting Ry in other ways. Given Ry's vulnerable position, it wouldn't be hard for Miles to make financial or even legal trouble for him, if he wanted to.

Which reminded her that Margaret, no doubt, would be vigilant this morning, as she always was. She would have to speak to her, and make sure that word of this particular visit didn't reach Miles's ears.

Thinking hard, she padded, naked, to the bathroom.

Very few men would have been able to watch Ginny with indifference as she stepped into the shower. Her body was a glimpse of smooth, sculptural perfection. Since she had lately not bothered with the vanity of tanning, her skin was creamy-pale, flawless but for the pink tips of her breasts, and the dark smudge at her loins. With long, beautiful legs, and breasts that were high and firm, she moved with almost balletic grace. Everything about her was exquisitely formed, the slender column of her throat, the sensual oval of her mouth, the dark star of her navel.

She soaped her smooth skin, rinsing away the fading terrors of the night. But her thoughts had turned down an avenue that was, if anything, even darker than her nightmare had been.

Miles's revelations had been horrible. Yet she couldn't honestly say she'd expected anything else of Ry. She hadn't really believed Ry when he'd said he was changed, had she? No, of course not. She wasn't that gullible.

Yet she cared so much for Ry. Couldn't something be done for him? But who was there who could help him?

She was on the verge of tears as she emerged from the shower, reaching blindly for her towel. She dried herself, but instead of getting dressed, went to the window wrapped in her towel, and sat in the window-seat, looking out.

It was still very early, not even six o'clock yet. Complete silence sat over the world, hardly even a bird stirring in the clear skies above.

Something more then Ry's dream-image had died during the night; the last of her illusions about him, herself and Miles had died too. The hot confusion of being with Ry had subsided; but so too had the idealised illusion she'd been living in since trying on her wedding dress. Suddenly, Ginny was seeing things with a cool clarity which she'd never had before.

She didn't love Miles Langton.

She never had done. Her feelings towards him had been of gratitude and respect. Maybe even affection. But never, not even for an hour, of love.

She had only loved one man in her life, and she would only ever love one man. And that was Ry Savage.

She'd tried to forget him. For a couple of years, she'd even succeeded. But from the moment he'd reappeared in her life, she'd been lost again, as much Ry's slave as she'd been as a sixteen-year-old schoolgirl, all those years ago.

So where did that leave her? Out of love with the man she was due to marry in a fortnight's time. And hopelessly enslaved by a man who was totally unacceptable as a husband in almost every way. Except one—that he was the most beautiful man she would ever see.

A great weariness had settled over Ginny. Her heart was aching for Ry, for herself. What was she going to do? Could she still marry Miles, given what she had now recognised about herself?

I love you. She'd never said those words to Miles. There had been moments when she'd wanted to say them, but shyness, or reserve, had kept them unsaid.

And now she was having to realise that she had agreed to marry Miles out of motives which didn't include love. Motives which she could now hardly understand any more, but which had been compelling enough at the time to make her accept his offer, and believe that she was doing the right thing.

Did Miles know she didn't really love him? She'd covered the fact by a hope that love would come to her, once they were married, once they were sleeping together, and once she had a child. But in the unbearably clear light of this morning, Ginny knew that that hope was a thread delicate as gossamer on which to suspend a marriage.

He must surely know that she wasn't burning with passion for him, that she didn't find him physically attractive. But then he wasn't that sort of man. He was about the least physical man she knew. Maybe it was that very factor that had enabled the whole thing to get this far . . .

She wondered remotely whether Miles's feelings for her were as abstract and colourless as her feelings for him. If they were not, then she would be doing something very, very wrong in marrying him.

And what about her own point of view? Could she really marry a man she didn't love?

A bitter smile crept across her full mouth. Of course she could. Millions of women were married to men they didn't love, but who could provide security, a home, a family.

The question was whether she was one of those women, whether she wanted that kind of marriage. Whether she could endure the lifetime that stretched out ahead of her.

She'd learned a lot about Miles, yesterday. She'd learned that there was a lot more to him than the mild, honourable man she'd always respected. He was capable of manipulative, unscrupulous behaviour to get what he wanted.

I have influence, that's all I mean. All sorts of influence.

Yes. It was so easy for a bank manager in a small town to exert that influence. So easy for him to grant or withdraw favours that would never be noticed by the bank, but which meant so much to the people concerned —extending overdrafts, granting loans, easing repayment terms . . .

That was how he stayed so popular, so respected. That was how he had made Margaret his spy all this time. And God knew what Ry had said to Margaret that night when she'd slept at her mother's. It didn't bear thinking of.

What with one thing and another, she owes the bank a favour, as you might say.

How many other people owed Miles Langton similar favours?

Ginny got up stiffly, feeling years older than her twenty-one. She had to face herself with brutal honesty. Given that she couldn't marry the only man she ever would love, was Miles Langton any worse or better than anyone else? After all, he was not corrupt. Just determined. And ruthlessness was not an undesirable quality in a husband, was it?

But that was a callous thought. She dressed slowly. She would have to talk this through with Miles, as soon as possible. She'd told him a lot of lies yesterday—not because she'd wanted to deceive him, but because at that stage she hadn't faced the truth herself yet. But now it was important that she tell him exactly what her feelings were, and give him a chance to withdraw from this marriage, if that was what he wanted. He'd said he'd been on the edge of breaking everything off yesterday, so he'd clearly been as full of doubts as she had.

I was on the edge of cancelling our engagement this morning.

What had that emotion been that had twisted through her heart when he'd said that? Alarm? Relief?

Why *had* she agreed to marry him? To be mistress of Greenlawns? Wry amusement made her smile to herself again. That was something she would never be, not while Jessica Langton was alive. In any case, social standing had never been something she cared about.

For the money, then, the way Ry had always accused her?

Perhaps there had been more truth in that bitter accusation than she had ever admitted. Perhaps she *had* been dazzled by the prospect of being a rich woman, of having the security that wealth could bring.

In the wake of Ry's departure for London, she'd gone through a phase of deep insecurity that had reawakened all the fears dormant in her since her father's death. Perhaps she'd realised, even then, that Ry was never going to be her husband, and that she would never want anyone else. Otherwise, she would never have even contemplated Miles Langton as a husband, because although she respected and liked him as a friend of the family, she did not love him, and never would.

But she knew what Miles could offer her. In the absence of love, security was a good second. In a small town, in a predominantly rural county, an offer of marriage from a man like Miles Langton meant a great deal. It had meant enough to make her say yes without regret or hesitation.

Two weeks. A fortnight, and she would be married. Ginny felt a wave of panic rise in her, making her fingers tremble as they fastened her buttons. What if her cool logic was just folly, and it was all a horrible mistake? It was like being on an escalator that was going the wrong way, carrying her to a destination she no longer wanted to reach.

With a chill, Ginny realised that the image had come from her nightmare at the cottage. She fought down the

strong beauty that melted her heart.

Ginny looked away from him, fighting down her emotions. 'Whatever the rights and wrongs of yesterday,' she went on, 'Miles knows about you and me.' She laughed with a catch in her voice. 'That sounds so guilty, doesn't it? I mean that he knows you've been seeing me, and that you've been trying to talk me out of marrying him. He told me that he was on the verge of breaking off our engagement yesterday.'

Ry rolled over, looking at her with deep, shrewd eyes. 'Is that so?' he drawled lazily.

'He was very upset. And I've been horribly upset lately too. There've been times when I didn't think I could go on any further. And yesterday just put the lid on it.'

'In what sense?'

'In the sense that I've had to face a great deal, Ry. About myself. About Miles. And about you.'

'Go on.'

'I said I'd be brief,' she said with a painful smile. 'So here goes. About myself—I don't have any more illusions, not about anything. In the past couple of years, I've changed out of the girl you used to know into somebody very different. Somebody who doesn't believe in romance any more. Somebody who's pragmatic, even cold-hearted, if you like. But someone who knows what she wants out of life.'

'You sound as though you don't like the new Ginny Northcliffe very much,' Ry commented sardonically.

'No, I don't think I do.' Ginny tugged restlessly at the grass beside her. 'But I have to live with her. Anyway, so much for me. I don't really want to talk about myself any more. Now to Miles.' She took a deep breath. 'You were right, Ry. I don't love him—I never have done. It took you to show me that.'

Ry's eyes glittered. 'Thank God for that!'

'I don't love him,' she went on in a monotone, 'but I do respect him. And I think I still want to marry him.'

Ry's curse was explosive. 'For God's sake, Ginny! How can you be such a little fool?'

'We're both fools, aren't we?' she asked tiredly. 'Me in my way, you in yours. But I mean what I say. I accepted Miles's offer of marriage when he first made it, and I stand by that. I shall have to tell him that I don't love him,' she went on, dropping bits of grass from her fingers. 'I owe him that much. But I think he'll accept that. And I think he'll still want me.' She met Ry's fierce gaze, and shook her head slightly. 'You were right when you said I didn't love him. But deep down, it doesn't really make that much difference. I'm not marrying him for love.'

'No,' grated Ry. 'You're marrying for money.'

Ginny opened her mouth to retort, then thought better of it. 'You may be right,' she shrugged. 'I'm not going to argue about it any more. Whatever happens between me and Miles is our business, and no one else's. And you, of all people, don't have the right to criticise the way I behave.'

'OK,' said Ry, obviously keeping calm with an effort. 'Which brings you to me. What great truth have you learned about me in the past twenty-four hours?'

'Nothing I didn't know already,' she said with an attempt at a smile.

She'd already decided that she would say nothing about what Miles had told her yesterday. It would be too cruel, and would serve no purpose. But she'd made up her mind to be blunt with him, for his sake as well as for hers.

'We've been friends a long time,' she said unevenly. 'More than friends. It's been beautiful, Ry—I mean that. But now it must end. It *has* to end. It can't go on, not under the circumstances. I'm saying that I don't—I don't want to—to ever see you again.'

God, that had been hard to say. It had sounded so easy as she'd rehearsed it in her bedroom this morning. But now that it had come to uttering the words, with Ry's blue eyes on hers, her resolve was crumbling like a sandcastle under the surf.

Suddenly she was fighting against the tears that blinded her, and turned the river into a blurred sheet of stars. She couldn't go on, and she bit her lower lip to stop it trembling.

Ry made no effort to touch her or comfort her. Instead, he said in a calm voice, 'And what if the circumstances change? Supposing Brother Miles decides he doesn't want a wife who doesn't love him, and who never will? Will you want to see me again then?'

Ginny shook her head, still incapable of speaking. Her throat was aching with grief, and she was desperately trying not to give way to racking sobs.

'So you expect me to conveniently vanish out of your life? Having told me that you don't love Miles Langton, do you really think I'm going to just fade away?' He sounded almost amused. 'This is only the half-way point, my love.'

Ry watched her for a moment, but she was hiding her face in her arms, too upset to respond. He rose to his feet and walked down to the river, and stood there a long time with folded arms, watching the water, lost in thought. Ginny fought down her tears, controlling herself with an effort, and raised her head to look at him. He was tall and straight against the sunlit water, his figure suggesting, even in repose, the tremendous energy he was capable of.

Again, Ginny had that vision of him standing with little Lucy in his arms, and again that sad thought—how could someone so gifted have gone so wrong?

He turned, and caught her watching him. As he walked back up to her, he was smiling slightly.

'OK,' he said, sitting down beside her again, 'you've had your say. Now I'll have mine. And what I have to say won't take long either. Are you in a fit state to listen?'

'Yes,' she said, wiping her eyes.

'All right. I'm glad you've finally started facing yourself about Miles, though you've obviously got a long way to go yet. The trouble is that we don't have much time any more. You're getting married in a fortnight.' His eyes were very serious, more serious than she'd ever seen them before. 'I know you blame me for leaving you the way I did. You think I don't really care about you. As it happens, I never stopped thinking about you while I was in London. And I missed you a great deal—more than you, with your silly misconceptions about me, could ever guess at. But I want you to believe that I was very, very busy during those years, and that I would have come for you much sooner, if I'd felt able to.'

'Oh, I'm so flattered to hear that,' she said bitterly, but Ry ignored the interruption.

'A few weeks ago there was a breathing-space in my life, and I knew that it was time to see you again. When I came back to Grantley, my intentions were firm. I knew what I wanted to say to you.' He smiled slightly. 'But I didn't bank on having to say it so soon. And I certainly didn't bank on finding you engaged to Miles Langton.'

'No,' she agreed, dry-eyed now. 'You thought I'd be waiting patiently for you, for the rest of my life!'

'I'm an arrogant pig,' he nodded, 'I fully agree. I guess I *did* expect you always to be there. I thought all I had to do was ask you to wait. Not quite the attitude a man should have towards the woman he loves.'

Ginny looked up at those words, and met his eyes. There was no mockery in them, no irony, and she felt her heart start to thud heavily in her chest.

Ry reached out and touched her cheek with gentle fingers. 'I'm reforming, Ginny, like I told you. I'm changing all the time. It isn't easy for someone like me to alter his ways, but I am doing it—I promise you that. I've already changed from what I was, changed out of all recognition. You can't see it yet. Or perhaps you just don't want to see it. But it's true, all the same.'

What Miles had told her yesterday flashed through her thoughts, filling her with ironical disbelief. 'If you mean that you've got more money to throw around these days,' she said acidly, 'I would hardly call that a significant change.'

'Nor would I,' he agreed calmly. 'But I don't mean that. As I told you once before, that kind of success means very little to me. The achievement of a man like Miles Langton, consisting mainly of accumulating a great deal of money, is ultimately meaningless. It fills me with contempt.'

'You're right—you *are* arrogant,' she said shortly. 'But it's easy to despise what you can't have, isn't it?'

'Making money is easy,' he retorted. 'You'd be surprised just how easy it is. All it requires is the right attitude towards your fellow-man.' His eyes were piercing. 'There are other kinds of achievement, things that matter more than money.'

'I see,' she said nastily. 'You've gone in for the spiritual life, have you? And what towering achievement can you report on, Ry?'

His fingers supped her chin, tilting her face up so that her unwilling eyes met his again. 'I love you, Ginny,' he said quietly, ignoring her petty comment. 'I want you to forget all about Miles Langton. I want you to marry me.'

CHAPTER NINE

GINNY felt her face freeze in shock and disbelief at what Ry had said. She could only stare at him, her mind numb. Then, without thinking, she slapped him across the face as hard as she could. She was swinging at him a second time when he caught her wrist in strong fingers, stopping her. Her eyes had flooded with tears again, and when at last she found her voice, it was trembling with pent-up emotion.

'Damn you, Ry!'

'Take it easy, darling.'

'You bastard!' She choked on the words. 'Why didn't you say that five years ago, before all this happened?'

'You'll see why, one day.' He kissed her trembling mouth with warm lips. 'The important thing is that I'm saying it now. We've always loved each other, right from the start. You can't marry Miles Langton—the idea is obscene, Ginny. You were born to love *me*. You don't have any choice but to marry me.'

'Marry you?' She pushed him away, the pain almost too sharp for her heart to bear. 'I might have been fool enough to marry you, five years ago. I'm not any more!'

'Why not?' Ry's voice was gentle. 'Have you really stopped caring for me, Ginny darling?'

'You fool,' she said harshly. 'I care for you more than you've ever deserved!'

'But?' he prompted.

'But you're in no position to marry anyone, least of all me.' She forced herself to speak calmly, despite the turmoil in her heart. 'How can you talk of marriage? You have nothing to commit to any woman.'

'I have myself,' he said quietly. 'Isn't that enough?'

'And what are you?' Ginny retorted. 'A drifter, a gypsy. Someone who's here one day, and gone the next, someone who refuses to conform to any rules.' She glared at him with hot brown eyes. 'What have you got to offer a wife? A life on the back of your motorbike, wandering from pillar to post? An existence of dishonesty and laziness? You're wasting your life, Ry. Asking any woman to marry you is asking her to waste the rest of her own life with you!'

He watched her with calm eyes. 'There was a time when you'd have felt differently about spending your life with me.'

'A long time ago.' She brushed the hair away from her eyes, her fingers shaking. She was getting over the shock of Ry's offer of marriage, and was feeling anger start to burn inside her, bright and hot. How could he do this to her, how *could* he? Of all the cruel, dirty tricks . . . 'In any case,' she gritted, 'I know perfectly well that there isn't an ounce of sincerity in what you say. You're exactly as serious about marrying me as you are about buying that Maserati you once wanted so badly!'

'All right.' His face was calm. 'Let's say I deserve all the reproaches and rebukes you can throw at me. But let's also assume that I'm quite serious about wanting to marry you. Serious enough to go through with it tomorrow, if needs be. What reason have you got for refusing me?'

Something in the tone of his deep voice made her hesitate, her anger fading.

'Good sense, that's what. I've grown up, Ry,' she said, more quietly. 'You can mock my need for security, but it's very real. A woman has to be practical about these things, because life isn't like the movies. Making a mistake in the man you marry doesn't just mean misery for you, but for the children you bring into the world too. Can you say that you could provide the right environment to bring up a child?'

'I can say that a child of mine would be loved and cared for as well as any child in England,' he said quietly.

'That's not enough.' Ginny looked away from those deep, searching eyes. 'Can't you see that it's not Miles's money that means so much to me? It's his sense of duty, his sense of responsibility. It's knowing he's an honourable man who will give his children security and comfort, and be a father they can always look up to!'

'You really have grown a set of sharp nails,' he murmured. 'Do I truly seem so irresponsible to you, Ginny?'

'Yes!' she snapped.

'Why? Because I wear an earring and leathers, and ride a motorbike—instead of gliding to work in a Jaguar, wearing a grey three-piece suit?'

'Because you don't have a regular jop,' she said sharply. 'Because you're involved in God knows what misdemeanours up in London. Because you don't have enough pride not to debase yourself by labouring on a farm, or running other people's errands in other people's cars!'

'You little snob,' Ry said softly, his eyes narrowing to smoky slits in his bronzed face. 'What the hell is so wrong with turning an honest penny on a farm? Or running errands for someone, come to that? Are you so damned high and mighty that nothing short of a bank manager will do you?'

'Don't sneer at me,' she said tightly. 'You have no right to!'

'Of course I have the right to,' he said explosively. 'You're trying to tell me that the sweet, lovely girl I used to know has turned into a status-hunting, gold-digging, mercenary little hireling, and I refuse to believe it!'

'I've had just about *enough* of being called mercenary,' she said fiercely. 'It's bad enough getting it from Miles and Jessica's cherished friends the whole time. I don't need *you* to add to the chorus!'

'It sounds to me like a case of the Emperor's new clothes,' Ry commented drily. 'Everyone can see the truth except you.'

'Cheap shot!'

'Tell me,' he went on sarcastically, 'what makes you so sure your precious Miles is such an honourable man? The fact that he owns a Jag and a mansion, and has a big job in a small pond? We're talking about the man who set your neighbour to spy over you, remember. Miles Langton doesn't know what warmth or affection are. Have you still not realised what a cold, deceitful little nonentity he really is?'

'Ry, stop it!' she snapped.

'All right.' His mouth was grim. 'We'll forget Miles for the time being. Let's just talk about you and me, because there's another question you haven't answered. Can you look me in the eyes and tell me you don't love me?'

Ginny felt the hot flush suffuse her cheeks. 'The truth is——' she began, but ran out of words.

'The truth is?' he prompted.

'I—I once felt a—a—great deal for you,' she said, unable to look him in the face. 'But I was so much younger then—just a teenager. I was hardly seventeen when you left for London.' At last she raised her eyes to his. 'Seventeen, Ry. That was five long years ago. How many times have you come to see me in those five years?'

'Too few times,' he said gently, his expression compassionate.

'Too few times,' she nodded. 'And you let almost two years go by since the last time you came to see me. So much water has passed under the bridge in those years. We're like strangers now. We hardly know one another any more. It's foolish to talk about love.'

Ry's mouth curved into an unexpected smile. 'You do know,' he said huskily, 'that I just have to kiss you to prove that everything you've just said is completely wrong?'

'Ry,' she sighed, 'you're trying to make a river flow backwards. That just doesn't happen.'

'Feelings like ours don't die, darling. They just get stronger and stronger. Our love has had to wait. It's taken me five years to be able to ask you to marry me, and there've been reasons for that. Good reasons. Whatever else I've done, I've never lied to you. I'm asking you to believe me now. And you have to be equally truthful with yourself. You have to admit that this escapade with Miles Langton has been abnormal, an anomaly that could never have come true. You have to admit that you love me.'

'Why? To satisfy your ego?'

'No. Because it's the truth.' He cupped her face in his hands, searching her eyes with a smiling, deep blue gaze. 'I love you,' he said softly, his words seeming to reach deep into her heart. 'I've always loved you, Ginny. And now I've come back to you. You can't turn away from me, girl.'

His words had opened the floodgate of emotion inside her. Pain and love and desire were welling up in her, drowning her self-control. Tears were flooding her eyes again, spilling down her cheeks and over his fingers.

'Please,' she begged jerkily. 'Don't—do this—to me!'

Ry bent forward, and kissed the soft oval of her mouth with gentle intensity. 'Say it,' he commanded in a rough whisper. 'Tell me you love me.'

'No!'

'God knows I've waited long enough. Tell me!'

Frantic to get away, Ginny pushed him back, and got to her feet. Her heart was pounding in her ears, thudding against her ribs.

'I can see that it was a bad mistake to come here with you,' she said, choking back her tears. 'Take me home, Ry. I've got nothing more to say to you.'

'But I've got plenty more to say to *you*,' he growled, also getting up, and towering over her like a thundercloud.

'Write me a letter,' she jerked out bitterly. 'And don't bother giving me a lift—I'll walk.'

She turned away and started stalking blindly up the bank.

Ry's fingers closed round her elbow with enough force to really hurt, and he swung her round to face him. 'Damn you,' he said softly. 'I've got a good mind to——'

Ginny glared into his smoky blue eyes. 'Let me go!'

'So you can run back to your sugar-daddy?' he said scornfully. 'Do you think his money will help you forget me, Ginny? Do you think his lovemaking could ever satisfy you—always assuming he's got the manhood to actually manage anything in bed beyond dreaming of his pension?'

Shock made her blanch. 'How *dare* you talk to me like that!'

'Oh?' He tilted an eyebrow at her. 'Can you tell me otherwise?'

'I can tell you,' she spat out, 'that Miles Langton is a better lover than you'll ever be!'

For a moment Ry just stared into her eyes, his face taut with anger. Then, with something suspiciously like a grim smile, he pulled her forward, his strength vast and effortless.

Before she knew what he was doing, he had hoisted her on to his shoulder, and Ginny's world had turned upside down, her hair tumbling over her face and eyes.

She gave a strangled yelp, and pounded his muscular back with her fists, which produced about as much effect as hitting a granite boulder.

With a flash of horror, she realised that he was carrying her down to the river.

'Ry!' she gasped, *'no!'*

But Ry ignored her protests utterly. He paused for a moment, shifting her weight in his arms, and then she felt herself catapulted through the air.

She plunged into the water with a cold, crashing shock, and found herself sinking to the oozy bottom. Water had been driven up her nose, and there was hardly any air in her lungs, probably because she'd screamed as he'd tossed her into the river. Ginny panicked, floundering in the reeds, feeling the wet strands of duckweed clinging to her face and hands. For a horrible moment she thought she'd never make it to the air again, and then she saw the silver surface glimmering above her.

She broke the surface with a gasp of spray, caught a glimpse of Ry, standing on the bank, then almost instantly started sinking again. It was unexpectedly deep and cold, and her clothes were clinging heavily around her limbs, dragging her down. Besides, she had the awful feeling that she was ensnared in weeds, being enmeshed in the fronds of reeds and bulrushes.

She fought frantically to the surface again, and got her head out of water for a moment.

'Ry! Help!'

Then she was going down again, the cold dark water enfolding her. She was just about to despair when strong arms reached round her, hauling her upwards. He had dived in after her. Choking and coughing, she let Ry tow her to the bank.

She tottered upright in the shallows, helped by Ry's firm hands, and turned to glare at him.

'You might have drowned me!' she spluttered, still unable to believe he'd really thrown her in.

'You used to be such a good swimmer,' he said mildly. Water was pouring off him, soaking his shirt to his hard torso. 'Besides,' he added, 'you shouldn't have been so bitchy.'

Ginny groaned, and wiped the sodden hair away from her face. She clambered up the bank and looked down at her drenched, weed-strewn self. 'My God,' she sighed. 'What am I going to do?'

Ry was laughing softly as he waded up to her. 'You'd better get those wet things off, and let them dry.'

'What—and sit around in my underwear with you?' she scorned.

'Why not? It's what we used to do.'

'Not any more,' she said firmly, and tried to wring the water out of her shirt-front.

'I enjoyed that,' smiled Ry. 'Maybe you're in a better mood to listen now?'

'I'm listening,' she said ironically. 'Just don't throw me in again.'

Ry was close to her. 'This is all I wanted to say.' He kissed her wet mouth, his arms drawing her close to him. It was an achingly sweet moment, and as he drew back, she looked up at him with soft brown eyes.

'God, you're so beautiful,' he whispered. His mouth closed on hers again, with a fierce ardour that overwhelmed her. For a moment she struggled in his arms; this was wrong, disastrous! But it was better than thinking any more. And it was so good to let all the pain and confusion dissolve into the melting-pot of passion, so sweet to give way to Ry, and let him push her back among the grass at the river's edge.

There was the same consuming intensity in his kiss as there had been that afternoon at her flat, the same elemental desire in him. But this time there was a gentleness too, a tenderness that seemed to melt her, like honey in the sun.

As she slid her arms around his neck, she felt once again that strange combination of aliveness and dreaminess, of being both remote and vividly aware of every sensation—the slippery provocation of his tongue, the sweet smell of his wet skin and hair, the feel of his man's body so close and possessive against hers.

Nothing in her life, she now knew, affected her so much as Ry's touch. *He's right,* she thought dreamily. *I do love him. I've always loved him . . .*

All that had changed over the past five years was that her feelings had matured, grown stronger and deeper than anything a sixteen-year-old could have felt.

Her mouth opened to his kiss. It didn't matter any more that she was soaked to the skin, that her clothes were almost certainly wrecked. All that mattered was Ry holding her, kissing her . . .

It seemed to take a long time to get to the other end of the tunnel. Ages later, she opened her drugged lids to see him smiling down at her.

'I love you,' he said gently.

Such beautiful words. Ginny closed her eyes, holding up her mouth to be kissed again, but he laughed.

'Let's go in again.'

'Oh, no . . .'

'I mean properly, the way we used to do in the old days. We're both filthy with weeds. There's a much cleaner stretch of river beyond the willows.'

'Someone might see us . . .'

'No one ever comes here,' he smiled. 'No one knows about this place except us. We can leave our clothes to dry in the sun while we swim. In this heat, they'll be at least wearable in a while.'

Not waiting to argue, Ry started stripping his clinging shirt off. Suddenly absurdly shy, Ginny fumbled with her own buttons. It would be good to get the soggy things off, and rinse her naked skin in the cool water, after all. It was surprisingly hard to get wet clothes off, and she wriggled awkwardly out of her blouse.

'Come on!'

She glanced up at Ry, and felt her heart tighten with shock. He was already undressed, laughing down at her. She'd never seen him completely naked before, and in the hot sunlight he was an image of potent male perfection. His body was etched with muscle, tapering from wide shoulders to hard, lean hips and muscular thighs. The only part of his skin which wasn't tanned a deep mahogany was a narrow strip across his loins, which seemed to emphasise his sexuality.

She heard his soft laughter. 'Come and join me when you're ready.' He walked a little way down the bank, and plunged cleanly into the water, then swam outward.

Her own body was so much paler than his when she'd shed the last of her clothes. In the sunlight, her skin glowed like ivory, as beautifully female as his body was male. Her nipples were tensed and proud, the curves of her body sensual yet slender. There was no excess fat to mask the healthy, dancer's frame as she walked along the bank to where Ry had dived in.

She hung her wet things over a bush next to Ry's, and followed him into the water. Here the bottom was sandy and free of weeds, and the flowing water was crystal-clear. She struck out as soon as she was beyond the shallows.

This time the shock of coldness was welcome, spreading cleanly between her thighs and around her breasts. Cutting across the gentle current, she paddled out after Ry.

He was waiting for her underneath a long, outstretched willow-branch, hanging on to the tree with one arm. It was, she recognised at once, a favourite spot of theirs from long ago. She joined him, reaching up to hold on to the same branch.

'I remember this place!'

'I thought you would.' His eyes dropped to her breasts, just visible beneath the water, but she felt no shyness now.

'I didn't mean to misbehave myself so dramatically this morning. Some of the things you said just . . . upset me.'

'Some of them were meant to,' he said wryly.

She smiled. 'I've found I can still swim, anyway. Race you to the other side?'

He beat her easily, and she was panting as she came in a poor second. He was waiting for her in the silvery shallows, reaching for her hand. They idled in the cool water, getting their breath back.

Ginny looked across the river. It was so beautiful, so tranquil. So good to be here with Ry again, naked in the water, feeling the slow current tugging at them, wanting to carry them downstream, down to the distant sea. If only they could let go, and just drift together, towards that far horizon . . .

'Sorry,' smiled Ry at last, meeting her eyes. 'It wasn't very gallant of me to throw you into the river.'

'It wasn't very clever of me to say what I did,' Ginny replied. She hesitated, but only for a moment. 'It wasn't true, anyway. Miles and I have never made love.'

'I know,' Ry nodded. His black hair had been slicked back from his water-beaded face, making him look younger, deceitless.

'I've only loved one man in my life,' she went on gently. 'I've loved him ever since I could remember.'

She had come a long way to this point. In the past couple of years, she had forgotten many things. Forgotten just how much she felt for Ry Savage. Forgotten that he was the most beautiful, marvellous man she would ever know. Forgotten how much a part of her he would always be.

'And this morning,' she said, turning back to him, 'I've found out that I still love him.'

Ry just reached for her, drawing her close to him. Their naked bodies clasped in the cool water, and Ginny closed her eyes in ecstasy. To feel his naked length against her was wonderful, erotic, yet also tender and innocent.

He kissed her face softly, carefully, his lips brushing her closed eyelids as though they'd been the softest petals.

'I'm glad you're so beautiful,' he said huskily. 'I'd hate to be this hopelessly in love with a gargoyle.'

Ginny opened smiling brown eyes. 'Would you still love me if I were a homely kid with buck teeth and pigtails?'

'You forget,' he reminded her, 'I *did* love you as a homely kid with buck teeth and pigtails.'

'I never had buck teeth!' she protested indignantly, and snuggled close against his muscular nakedness. 'Was that really what it was?' she wondered. 'Love? Can kids of that age really feel love?'

'We did,' he smiled, touching her lips with his fingers. 'As a matter of fact, you were fourteen when I first realised I was crazy about you.'

'Fourteen!' she laughed. 'You must have been all of eighteen at the time. Weren't you cradle-snatching a bit?'

'No. You were already the local beauty. To me, you were the loveliest girl in the world. Besides——' he brushed her breasts, almost as if by accident '—you were an early developer.'

She smiled. 'Was I?'

'I remember seeing you in a tight sweater one day,' he nodded. 'I had to sit down in a hurry.'

'Ry!' she gurgled with laughter.

'That means I've loved you for nearly eight years. It never occurred to me that I would ever love anyone else.'

Ginny looked up into his face, her smile fading. 'You really meant it, when you asked me to wait for you, didn't you?'

'Yes,' he nodded, 'I really meant it.'

'I didn't know . . . Maybe I believed you at first. Then my faith in you faded away. I thought you'd just stopped caring.'

'I never stopped caring. I always knew that I'd marry you. I just had this crazy idea that I should make something of myself first, and then come back for you. I see now that I should have kicked off by marrying you first, as soon as you were of age.'

'Oh, Ry,' Ginny sighed miserably, 'it's such a

horrible, confused mess . . .'

'My feelings aren't confused in the slightest,' he smiled. 'I want you. Simple as that. Every inch and ounce and ell of you.'

He kissed her mouth, hard. She felt his hand slide up to cup her breast, his fingers capturing the jutting nipple. Pleasure fluttered through her, and she felt the unmistakable surge of his response. She pushed away from him gently.

'No,' she said in a low voice, 'not now. Let's get back, Ry. I'm starting to feel cold.'

When they reached the other bank, their clothes were still soaked.

Ry surveyed his sodden shirt and slacks with distaste. 'Good job I brought my leathers. What are you going to do?'

'I'll be all right till I get home.' She did her best to make her jeans and shirt presentable; they were, however, in a sorry state. Ry zipped his naked body into the leather suit, and wrapped his clothes in a bundle. Putting on her own wet things gave Ginny a depressing sense of getting back to the real world, after a beautiful escapade. It was almost like putting on a convict's uniform again.

It occurred to her that she was due to meet Miles in a few hours. Would she be able to face him? And then the long afternoon at the Witherburns' . . .

She shook the revulsion away. The dream wasn't over yet. There was time enough to think about Miles later.

When they were dressed. Ry turned to her. 'We haven't finished talking yet, Ginny.' He took her hands, looking into her face. 'Let's play a game called *what if*. What if I got work, the kind of thing you'd call a decent job. What if I saved up and bought an acceptable flat in London, or maybe a house near here, in the country. What if I stopped living the footloose life you object to so much, and settled down to a family. What if I took up my responsibilities and social obligations, and all the rest of it.' He smiled at her expression. 'What if I promised I would do all that, or at least try my damnedest to do it all. Would you marry me then?'

Ginny stared up at him in silence, her stillness giving no sign of the turmoil inside her. If only he knew what those words did to her! They filled her heart with joy and terror. They made nonsense of all her resolutions, of all that she had believed about herself.

'*What if* is a game I've never liked,' she said unevenly. 'Maybe I've never understood it.'

'All right.' His eyes were deep, clear as the summer sky above. 'I'll put it more directly than that. If you'll marry me, Ginny, I promise you'll never regret it. I'll get a good job, I'll buy you a decent house to raise a family in, and I'll never leave your side as long as I live. Now,' he smiled, 'will you marry me?'

The coffee-cup splintered on the tiled floor of the kitchen. Hardly aware of what she was doing, Ginny stooped to sweep up the mess. Her hands were shaking so much that she was going to be lethal with crockery all day. Her mind was whirling with emotions, her thoughts as disjointed and broken as the shards of porcelain she was now throwing into the bin.

It seemed to be stiflingly warm in the flat, and she felt faint with the heat. The whirring of the washing-machine as it tumbled her river-drenched clothes seemed to be adding to her sensation of unreality. Despite the cool frock she'd put on, her skin felt clammy and prickly.

Pouring the coffee she'd just made into a fresh cup, she leaned against the cool surface of a kitchen cupboard and sipped the scalding fluid.

Had it been cowardice to temporise? To beg Ry for time, only a little time, to sort out her mind? Maybe. But what else could she have done?

How easy it would have been so simply say *yes* this morning. To have said *yes, I'll marry you,* and to have melted into Ry's arms at the riverside. The perfect ending to a romantic film. Cue for the credits to roll. Except that life, as she'd told Ry earlier on, was not like the movies.

The coffee was just making her hotter, and she abandoned it with a sigh, wandering through to the living-room, and pulling her freshly washed chestnut hair away from her steamy temples.

She was aching to see Ry again. It seemed like an eternity until tonight. He had promised to come to her again this evening, late, after she'd got back from Greenlawns. And privately, she had resolved that by then she would have an answer for him, one way or another.

The past few weeks had changed her life. Sometimes it went like that. Months and years drifted by with seemingly no change. And then, suddenly, everything that had been so secure and dull was turned on its head, and in the space of a morning, of a conversation, all was transformed, and the world was turned upside down.

The tension had been almost unbearable. Looking back over these past weeks, Ginny realised with a cold feeling just how close she had been to some kind of breakdown. Those horrible dreams that had so shaken her, those feelings of faintness and nausea—even the dizziness she now felt—had all been symptoms of powerful inner conflict. The way earthquakes and tremors were symptoms of contending frictions deep in the earth.

Well, now she could no longer ignore the warnings. Something had to give. Ry had skilfully driven her to a point where the truth had exploded around her. And today, now, she had to make her decision.

She felt that Ry was telling the truth about settling down and reforming; yet even if he wasn't, it didn't make much difference any more.

There was no reason that would stop her loving Ry. And she knew now in her heart that she could no longer face living out her life without him. Nothing else mattered beside that fact, not her engagement, not her life here in

Grantley, not even the shame and dishonour that she would surely bring on Miles's head if she were to cancel the wedding now, with the church booked, the dress almost made, and the invitations sent.

Ry had been right. She had been born to love him. Her dream that one day she would come to love Miles Langton was impossible. She would never love any man but Ry. Her feelings for him ran deep into her being, too deep ever to die. She had pruned the branches, yet the plant had just grown more powerfully and vigorously than before.

And this morning she had looked into his eyes, and had realised that he loved her. Loved her with the same helpless intensity and passion that she loved him.

Could she turn away from that?

Ry was wild and irresponsible, yes. She could almost find it hard to believe that he would ever settle to anything constructive. Yet there was so much more in him that she loved. No, not loved—adored. Worshipped, even.

His strength, that was so formidable, and yet tempered with so much gentleness. His confidence, the way he was always in control of every situation. His sexiness. The way he could always make her laugh. The way he excited her, the way his presence always made her heart beat faster and her breathing quicken. A thousand great and small things about him that she had always loved, that she would always love.

Things that no other man would ever have. Things for which she could easily put up with a little wildness. And she'd been so haughty towards him. How arrogant she'd been, how high and mighty! Another man, less in love with her and more in love with his own pride, would have stalked out on her ages ago!

If Ry wanted her to live the rest of her life on the back of a motorbike, then she would do it.

The photograph of Miles on the mantelpiece stared at

her, and she met its eyes with a wince.

Agreeing to marry Miles had been a desperate reaction against the fear that Ry would never come back for her. Thinking back, she could remember clearly her thoughts at the time of Miles's proposal.

She'd never tried to fool herself; ever since her dad's death, she'd been hungry for a mature male presence in her life, and that was exactly what Miles Langton provided. A father figure, to put it crudely. She'd known well in advance that Miles was going to ask her to marry him, and she'd had time enough to think out her response. The prospect of marriage to Miles had satisfied something deep inside her; how easy it had been to see herself as Mrs Langton, wealthy and respected, fearing nothing and wanting for nothing!

Pique against Ryan Savage had been another potent factor. By marrying Miles, Ry's antithesis in every way, she was cocking a snook at the hurt and insult she thought Ry had given her by abandoning her.

And the last element had been curiosity. Conceited, vain curiosity to see just what it would be like as the wife of a rich man, as the queen of Grantley society.

Looked at like that, it had been a monstrous misjudgment. How childish those three reasons now seemed, how mean and foolish her own behaviour. Yet at the time she'd felt so strongly that she was doing the right thing.

What a fool she'd been!

A feeling almost like self-hate had been burning in her all day. Could she ever make up for what she'd done? The thought of telling Miles that she wanted to cancel the wedding was almost unbearable.

Yet how could she think of going through with it, knowing that she loved Ry, knowing that she would effectively ruin three lives by marrying Miles?

She glanced at Miles's photograph again. There just wasn't a way round it. Whatever it cost, she was going to have to tell him she could no longer marry him.

As the decision crystallised, Ginny felt an extraordinary mixture of emotions rush through her heart. Terror at the prospect of confronting Miles's anger. Profound relief that she would not have to marry him. And joy that she would be Ry Savage's wife!

Tension released itself in the only way she knew how.

She was still crying softly when she heard the knock at her front door. It was early for Miles, but her heart was thudding as she rose from her chair, and tried to dry her eyes. She gathered all the courage she could muster, and went to the door.

But the person standing on the doorstep was Margaret Easy.

'What's the matter?' Margaret asked with unexpected urgency, seeing Ginny's tear-blurred eyes.

'Oh . . . it would be too complicated to explain.' She mopped her eyes with a hanky, and tried to smile. 'I was looking for you this morning.'

'I know. I heard you knock.' Margaret's pretty, rather heavy features were pale and tense, and her eyelids were swollen, almost as though she, too, had been crying that morning. 'I was still in bed. Can I come in?'

'Of course. Is something wrong?' asked Ginny, closing the door behind Margaret.

'Something's been wrong for a long time,' Margaret said dully. She sat, uninvited, in the chair Ginny had just vacated, and looked up at her, hugging her large bust. 'I've got to talk to you, Ginny. There's something I have to tell you, though you're not going to like it very much.'

Ginny looked at her quietly. 'All right,' she said, feeling that she knew what kind of confession was coming. 'Go on.'

Margaret took a deep breath. 'I don't suppose you've ever realised that I know Miles Langton quite well?'

'Well . . .' Ginny hesitated, then told the truth. 'I didn't until yesterday. You don't have to explain anything, Margaret. Miles told me that he'd asked you to—keep an eye on me.'

'To spy on you,' Margaret corrected savagely. 'I've never been fond of euphemisms—unlike your fiancé. So he told you?'

'Don't sound so bitter,' Ginny said gently. 'Yes, he told me. He also told me that you didn't have much choice in the matter. He put pressure on you.'

'Yes,' Margaret agreed drily. Ginny caught a strong gust of alcohol on her breath, and realised she'd been drinking. 'Miles is good at putting pressure on people. All sorts of pressure.'

'So I'm beginning to discover,' Ginny nodded. She sat down opposite Margaret. 'I'm glad you've told me. Please don't think I'm angry with you, or anything like that.'

Margaret gave her a bittersweet smile. 'You're such an innocent, Ginny. You really don't have the faintest idea what your fiancé is really like, do you?'

'I don't understand what you mean,' Ginny said, feeling uneasy.

'No, I don't suppose you do.' Margaret twisted her cigarettes and lighter between long, plump fingers, and looked down. 'Miles made me do a lot of things before he asked me to spy on you. I owe the bank a lot of money, you see. Besides the mortgage, I mean. I've taken out personal loans, HP agreements, a credit card, all sorts of mad things. When I lost my job, I was in bad trouble. I stood to lose the flat and everything in it. And the car. That's when Miles suggested we might come to some kind of—arrangement.'

'What sort of arrangement?' Ginny frowned.

'Be your age,' Margaret said shortly. 'What kind of arrangement do you think?' Her eyes glittered. 'You aren't *that* innocent, are you?'

Ginny felt suddenly cold. 'I don't believe you.'

'For God's sake, do you think it's easy for me to come in here and say all this?' Margaret lit a cigarette with unsteady fingers and blew a gin-scented cloud of smoke at the ceiling. 'What the hell would I lie for? It's the truth. Your precious Miles agreed to stop the bank foreclosing on me, and give me time to pay my debts off without losing everything I had. All I had to do was oblige him. That was his word, by the way. *Oblige.* How's that for a euphemism?' She shook her head, watching the colour drain from Ginny's face. 'I warned you that you wouldn't like it.'

Ginny was feeling sick to her heart. She knew Margaret wasn't lying. Miles was capable of doing it, she believed that now. She had never liked Margaret, had even despised her. But listening to her now, she felt nothing but the deepest pity for her. 'Go on,' she said quietly.

'Oh, it's all very regular,' Margaret said in a dry voice. 'We meet twice a week, at a flat he's got, a few streets from here. I hardly minded at first. I certainly didn't have any scruples—I'm not that sort of woman, as you probably know. It seemed a small price to pay, to keep my lovely flat, and all my lovely things. Twice a week isn't much, after all. It's less than the national average, isn't it?' She smiled without humour. 'Miles is rather less than the national average in more senses than one, I might tell you. Take my advice,' she said with sudden vehemence. 'Stick with that motorbike-riding boyfriend of yours. I know a real man when I see one. And that one's worth a thousand of Miles Langton.'

'Margaret, I'm so sorry,' Ginny said helplessly. A feeling of real abhorrence for Miles was growing inside her. How could he have done such a thing? How could he have been so cruel, so mean? 'I don't know what else to say.'

'No. There isn't anything to say. The only thing I really hated was having to pretend I enjoyed it.' Margaret stubbed the cigarette out, as though its taste had suddenly become polluted by some memory. 'Anyway, when you came to live here, he told me I had to add spying to my other duties. Not that getting engaged to you stopped his twice-weekly obligation with me. He's still at it, you know. Tuesdays and Fridays, regular as clockwork——'

'Please don't say any more!' Ginny pleaded, unable to bear it. Anger and grief struggled in her. And this was the man she'd once thought she loved and respected!

'Sorry. I forgot you're sensitive about these things. He's a cool one, though, isn't he? Can you imagine setting your mistress to spy on your fiancée?' Margaret laughed. '*Mistress* is my own little euphemism, by the way.' She looked at Ginny. 'Funny—I thought you'd be bursting with righteous indignation. The last thing I expected from you was sympathy.'

Ginny shook her head tiredly. 'Why should I be angry with *you?*'

'Because I've been a bitch—a complete, callous bitch. I've been sitting in my flat with a bottle of gin, thinking about what a swine Miles is, and what a bloody fool I've been to put up with him, and the upshot was that I realised I couldn't do it any longer.' There were suddenly tears in Margaret's eyes. 'I've just got to the end of my tether. I never thought I would, but I have. And I wanted you to know just what a bastard you're going to marry. I have to warn you. He'll ruin your life . . .' Margaret broke off in tears.

'I'm not going to marry Miles, Margaret.' Ginny's mouth was set with bitter anger. 'No, I made the decision before you told me all this. I thought I didn't feel anything for him, but now I know I do. I feel contempt and anger. And I feel so desperately sorry for you.' She took a deep breath. 'Ry wants me to marry him. I've loved him ever since I was a teenager, and he loves me. I'm going to break everything off with Miles.'

A look of real pleasure lighted Margaret's glistening blue eyes. 'God, how marvellous! That gorgeous man!' She laughed maliciously. 'And what a kick in the teeth for Miles Langton! By God, I'd give a thousand pounds to see his face when you tell him!' Her smile disappeared. 'Listen, though. I haven't got to the real reason I've come here and told you all this.'

'Which is?' Ginny asked.

'Miles was here this morning—around eleven o'clock, I would think. And he had Eddie Barnet with him.'

Ginny felt her sickness intensify. 'Who's Eddie Barnet?' she asked.

'You know—Big Eddie.' Margaret grimaced. 'Grantley's resident psychopath. He used to be Jack Tarrant's gamekeeper until he got the sack over that business with the school kids. Anyway, Miles seemed to know you wouldn't be here. He asked where you were, and like the good little spy I am, I told him you'd gone off with lover-boy.'

'Oh, no,' Ginny said dully.

Margaret studied her cigarette fixedly. 'The trouble is, Eddie Barnet really is a nasty piece of work. Miles left again with him in his Jag. He didn't say much, but he looked very angry. I reckon he could hurt your friend if he found him. That's what I wanted to warn you about—you and him.'

But Ginny was hardly listening any more. She got up in agitation, her heart pounding. A vision of Eddie Barnet was vivid in her thoughts. 'Psychopath' was not far off the mark. A big, savage-looking man who had always had a special detestation for Ry, ever since Ry's teenage poaching days, Big Eddie was notoriously violent. 'Then I've got to see Miles,' she said flatly. 'I've got to tell him that everything is over, and stop him from hurting Ry! He probably knows that Ry works over at Newton . . . they'll probably go there to look for him. I have to hurry! Margaret, can I borrow your car? Please?'

'Go ahead.' Margaret fished in her jeans pocket and tossed the keys of her Fiesta to Ginny. 'Do me a favour in return?'

'Anything,' said Ginny, grabbing her shoulder-bag.

Margaret smiled lopsidedly. 'I've run out of gin.'

'Help yourself.' Ginny pointed at the drinks cabinet, and ran out of the flat.

CHAPTER TEN

IT OCCURRED to Ginny as she started Margaret's Fiesta that Miles might just be at Greenlawns. It was worth a try, at any rate, before driving all the way to Lacon's farm. Her mind whirling with worries about Ry, she did a U-turn in the quiet street, and set off towards the Langton house.

Ten minutes later she was pulling up on the drive outside Greenlawns, amidst a spurt of gravel. Miles's Jaguar was not there. But Jessica's Mini was. And Jessica herself was in the garden, wearing a wide-brimmed straw hat. She had a basket slung over one arm, and was gathering roses. She stood perfectly still as Ginny got out of the car and ran up to her. On her face was a calm smile.

'I have no idea where my brother is,' she said, before Ginny had a chance to speak. 'I presume that's what you wanted to know? But I wouldn't waste my time looking for him, if I were you.'

'What do you mean?' Ginny asked breathlessly.

'I mean that it's all over.' Still smiling, Jessica Langton reached out and cropped a faded rose. It fell to the lawn like a severed head. 'A long, long farewell to all your greatness, and so forth.'

Ginny stared at the handsome, hard face. 'Are you talking about our engagement?'

Jessica laughed contemptuously. 'What engagement? *You* aren't engaged to anyone any more, child. Least of all to my brother Miles. Your precious engagement ended this morning, when you chose to fornicate with your lover down by the river, in full public view.'

Ginny went white. 'That's a lie!'

'How dare you call me a liar,' Jessica said in a silky, whiplash voice. And in that moment Ginny knew with a sudden revelation that this woman had always disliked and resented her. 'You contemptible, presumptuous little nobody! Did you really think you could be a Langton? I just thank God that Miles's eyes have been opened now, before it was much too late.'

Ginny laid a hand over her beating heart, as if to ease the pain there. 'If you really want to know, nothing happened between me and Ryan Savage this morning.'

'Of course not,' sneered Jessica. 'You lay naked in the arms of your former lover, and nothing happened!' The secateurs slashed.

'Who—who told Miles that—that I was down at the river?'

'Ah! You thought you were so safe down among the bulrushes, didn't you?' Jessica's expression was gloating as she severed the head of another rose. 'But there are eyes everywhere, child. Especially in Grantley. Eyes to see and tongues to speak. This particular pair of eyes belongs to a strange, rough man—a gamekeeper turned poacher, named Eddie Barnet. He happened to be out with his ferrets when he saw you and Mr Savage *au naturel*. He came at once to tell Miles what he saw.' Another rose fell to the earth. 'And to think I nearly sent him away when he came to the kitchen door! I would call him a violent, brutal man. But he's proved a useful instrument in Miles's hands. Miles has great talents in that direction, you see. The most unexpected people turn out to be useful instruments in his hands. And when he finds your gypsy lover, I'm sure Eddie will prove a most useful instrument again. After all, a punishment is required, don't you think?'

'Nothing will be solved by violence,' said Ginny speaking calmly with a great effort. 'Yes, everything is over between me and Miles. It was all a terrible mistake, right from the start. But please, you *must* tell me where to find Miles, Jessica, before something bad happens. For your brother's own sake, if not for Ryan Savage's!'

'I warned Miles against you, right from the start.' Jessica moved to the next rose bush, ignoring Ginny's entreaty completely. 'I knew he would end by making an utter fool of himself. I told him that if he insisted on marrying, after all these years, he should have chosen someone nearer his own age, not quite so pretty, and a great deal better off. All our friends agreed, of course. But then men are such fools, don't you think? Any half-way sensible woman can twist most men round her little finger.'

'Please, Jessica,' Ginny said urgently. 'It's vitally important that I speak to Miles before——'

'Yet you can't accuse me of prejudice,' Jessica went on, obviously taking a deep pleasure in what she was saying and doing. 'I gave you every chance to prove that you weren't just a little guttersnipe. I set tests for you, girl. And you failed every one.' She held out the basket of roses to Ginny. 'Hold this a moment, will you?'

Ginny took the basket numbly. 'What do you mean, *tests*? What did I fail?'

Jessica waded into the rose-bed to reach some tall white blooms, far back. 'I warned Miles that you would be completely out of your depth in any kind of sophisticated company,' she said conversationally. 'I said I could prove it. So I asked our friends to put pressure on you. Nothing unpleasant, just enough to flush out your true colours. And I told Miles not to interfere to protect you, just to watch and observe.' She clipped several long stems. 'To my mind,' she went on, 'you failed utterly, as I knew you would. You betrayed yourself for the low-bred, common little chit you really are, without dignity or poise. But Miles was infatuated with you. There was always some excuse for your lack of breeding. Men *are* such fools about women, even my brother.' She emerged from the rose-bed and confronted Ginny with eyes that glittered with dislike. 'But I assure you, he has finally seen the light.'

'I see.' Ginny was cold with inner anger. 'So I have you to thank for all the insults and snubs and rudeness I've had to put up with from your so-called friends?'

Jessica bared her teeth in a smile without warmth. 'Miles is unsuited to marriage, and that is the fundamental truth, is it not? He has me to care for him, after all. He has no need of a youthful, troublesome wife.'

'No,' Ginny said bitterly, thinking of Margaret, 'most of Miles's domestic wants seem to be taken care of already.'

'Exactly. Let me give you some disinterested advice, Gina. Save yourself a lot of unpleasantness, and just stay out of Miles's sight, for ever. When my brother returns, I'll tell him that I've seen you, and given you your *congé*.' Jessica reached out her hand for the basket. 'That would be the cleanest and most discreet way, don't you think?'

'I'm sure it would,' Ginny said tightly.

'And you will cease to appear at the bank. You were due to take leave in a short while, anyway. Well, your leave has been brought forward by a little.'

'I see.'

'Of course,' Jessica went on, 'there's no question of hiding the truth from the town. It will be made *absolutely* clear that no blame attaches on Miles's side. It's up to Miles whether he lets it be known exactly how atrociously you've behaved. I can make no promises on that score. I wouldn't hold out much hope, if I were you. But then you can hardly expect lenient treatment, can you?' She flapped her hand impatiently. 'My basket, please.'

Something seemed to explode inside Ginny. Without thinking, she flung the basket at Jessica. The older woman flinched in alarm as severed roses scattered around her.

'No,' Ginny said in a voice that shook with passion, 'I'm *not* poised or dignified! And I wouldn't be like your hateful friends for all the tea in China. I'm *young!* I'm twenty-one, and Miles is more than twice my age, and I should never, ever have agreed to marry him.' Her eyes were blazing so intensely that Jessica took an involuntary step backwards. 'As for your precious brother,' she went fiercely, 'my eyes have been opened to *him* too. I've never despised anyone so much in my life! He's a cold, unscrupulous, dishonest hypocrite who doesn't deserve to be the lowest clerk in his own bank!'

'You're mad,' Jessica said weakly.

'No. I *was* mad, but now I'm sane. You dare talk to me of telling the town how badly I've behaved? I've just been speaking to a woman who has been inhumanly abused by Miles for months! He has used his authority to take advantage of her in the most abominable, shameful way imaginable! And it doesn't end there.' Ginny was panting with anger and scorn, her cheeks as flushed as Jessica's were now white. 'If the bank had the faintest idea of how Miles behaved in Grantley, he wouldn't last a second. He'd be lucky not to end up in jail, which is what he deserves. So tell him *that,* Jessica! Tell all your wonderful friends too! And tell Miles that if he touches a hair on Ry Savage's head, I'll make sure he never dares show his face in this town for the rest of his life!'

Miles's voice was thin and cold. 'That won't be necessary.'

Ginny spun round to face Miles. He was standing on the lawn behind her, his face pale but expressionless. His brown Jaguar was parked by the house. She had been so wrapped up in her anger that she hadn't even heard him arrive.

'Miles,' Jessica said in a shaking voice, 'what is this child talking about?'

'Never mind,' Miles said tensely. He met Ginny's eyes, his mouth compressed to a thin grey line. 'I would strongly advise you not to repeat any of these wild accusations, Ginny——'

'Don't threaten me!' she retorted contemptuously. Had she really once agreed to marry this cold, calculating man, whose very presence now made her skin creep? 'I've just been speaking to Margaret Easy. There's nothing you could say or do that would matter a damn to me now, Miles. Where's your pet gorilla? And where is Ry?'

'Don't——' Miles stopped short after the clipped word, as though for once in his life he could find nothing appropriate to say.

'Don't expose you?' Ginny finished for him. Her eyes flashed. 'After what you've done to Margaret Easy, and God knows how many other helpless people? After the corrupt way you've behaved?'

'That's slander! You'll find it very hard to prove corruption. The woman was willing.' But his hand was trembling as he raised it to adjust his spectacles.

'Willing?' Ginny echoed with disdain. 'That's a very ugly lie, Miles. I wonder whether you'd be able to carry it off, if any of this ever became public knowledge?'

Miles flinched. He slid his hands into his jacket pockets to hide their trembling. 'There's no sense in our exchanging hostilities, Gina. I'm prepared to make a deal with you.'

'A deal?' Ginny shook her head. 'I don't want to hear any more about your kind of deals, Miles.'

'Nothing will be said on either side about why our marriage was cancelled,' said Miles in a fast monotone, as though not wanting to give her a chance to interrupt. 'We'll just call it a mutual decision, without rancour on either side. Nobody will be blamed. I'll make all the arrangements about cancelling the wedding. The newspapers, and so forth. And——' he hesitated, as though doing a mental calculation '—I'll see that five thousand pounds is in your account by Monday morning.'

'Miles,' Jessica gasped, 'you've lost your reason!'

Ginny had enough lightness in her to actually smile.

'Five thousand pounds? Is that all?'

'Ten,' Miles said swiftly, his eyes intent on hers.

'I wouldn't take a hundred and ten,' she said contemptuously. 'The person whose silence you have to buy is Margaret Easy's. Talk it over with her—next Tuesday, at your little rendezvous. Only one thing interests me, Miles, and that's Ryan Savage. Have you done anything to him?' As Miles hesitated, looking frightened, she stepped towards him, her voice rising. 'If you've hurt him——'

'No. Not yet——'

'What do you mean, *not yet?*' She was almost shaking him, watched by a thunderstruck Jessica.

'He's eating lunch at that sordid place—the Cuban Hat. We saw the motorbike there,' Miles said in a voice that quivered. 'Barnet is waiting for him on the road outside——'

'With your orders to beat him up?'

'To rebuke him.'

Ginny was already running back to the Fiesta. She started the engine, then looked out through the window. Miles and his sister were both watching her from the lawn, looking small and pale and frightened. She twisted the diamond ring off her finger and threw it towards them. 'I meant it,' she said quietly. 'If a hair of his head has been harmed——'

She accelerated hard towards the gates, gravel spraying from her tyres, all over the immaculate emerald green turf.

The drive to the Cuban Hat seemed interminable, and her nerves were wound to snapping-pitch. *To rebuke him.* What was Big Eddie's idea of a rebuke? If she could just get there in time to warn Ry——

But as she swung the Fiesta into the car park, her whole body seemed to jerk with shock. An ambulance was parked near the back entrance, surrounded by a milling group of people. Its blue light was flashing, flashing, exactly as it had done in her nightmare.

Except that this was a waking nightmare, a broad daylight nightmare. Parked nearby was a white police Granada, obviously called off the motorway.

Ginny pulled up as near to the ambulance as she could, and jumped out of the car, leaving the door swinging.

'What's happened?' she gasped to the nearest person in sight. A bearded, middle-aged man, he turned to her with a shrug.

'Hell of a fight—two big blokes. Looks like one of 'em's in a bad way.' He nodded at the ambulance doors, which were just closing. 'There he goes now.'

With a warning blip of its siren, the ambulance nosed through the crowd and sped off in the direction of Highgates Hospital.

Ginny stared after it, frozen to the spot. She was too numb to think, unable to move or speak.

Then she heard Ry's voice.

'Ginny!'

He was making his way towards her, a tall figure in black leather, his arms outheld. She flew into his arms, clinging to him with something like desperation.

'Oh, thank God!' she moaned, and looked up at him, oblivious of the curious faces all around. 'Thank God it wasn't you! Are you hurt, my darling?'

'A few bruises.' Ry's face was unsmiling, his blue eyes dark and sombre. 'What are you doing here?'

'I came to find you. That man saw us down at the river this morning—Miles set him on to attack you!'

'Ah.' Comprehension dawned in Ry's face. 'So that was it! Not that Big Eddie would have needed much setting on. He's an old enemy of mine . . . I thought he'd just done it out of spite.'

Ginny gave a little cry as she saw the big, swollen graze on Ry's cheekbone. 'You *are* hurt! What happened?'

'I still hardly know.' Ry shook his dark head, looking

slightly dazed. 'I was walking out of the back entrance when he came at me. He had some kind of iron club—a wheel-spanner, I think.'

She felt faint. 'Oh, Ry!'

'He would have half killed me if I hadn't seen him coming out of the corner of my eye. I got the first couple of blows, and managed to dodge the rest.' Ry shook his head slowly, and glanced down at his knuckles, which were cut and bleeding. 'I hit him, but I didn't mean him to fall like that.'

'Like what?' she whispered, hearing the distant, ominous wail of the ambulance.

'He cracked his head as he went down. And then he just lay there, with his eyes open, and blood everywhere.' Ry didn't take his eyes off hers as the two policemen closed in around him. 'I think I've killed him, Ginny.'

'Yes. Thank you for letting us know. I'll tell him.'

Ginny replaced the receiver and padded as quietly as she could back to the bedroom. It was going to be another beautiful day. The sky was a clear, pearly blue through the windows of her flat.

The noise of eight o'clock Monday morning bustle drifted in faintly from the street outside the archway, hardly audible inside the flat.

She slipped into bed, trying not to disturb Ry. But he turned to her, muscular brown arms reaching to pull her close against him.

'Damn,' she said gently, and brushed the thick black hair away from his eyes. 'I hoped the phone hadn't woken you. You need your rest after that knock on the head.'

'I know what I need,' he smiled. They kissed, tenderly, then with growing passion. Feeling the exquisite thrill of possession, Ginny laid her hand on the naked skin of his stomach, feeling the hard muscles, the exciting curls of crisp, dark hair. This was her man. The only man she would ever love.

'Don't you want to know who that was?' she said at last, drawing back, her breath coming more quickly.

'All I know,' growled Ry, 'is that after two nights in your bed, and not a carnal moment in sight, I'm going out of my mind for you!'

'You've been far too fragile for anything like that,' she smiled, touching the plaster on his cheek and looking down into his face. The most beautiful male face she would ever see, looking up at her with warm, incredibly deep blue eyes.

He laughed softly and started unfastening the ribbon that secured her prim white nightdress. 'Shall I show you just how un-fragile I am?'

'When we're married,' she said coolly, her fingers imprisoning his, 'you can show me . . . everything.'

'Then I want another kiss to be going on with.'

Her lips clung to his, her senses filled with the smell of his skin, the intoxication of his hard, warm body naked beside hers. When they were married. That was a thought that made even the agony of this sweet frustration worthwhile. When they were married . . . when they slept together like this, every night . . . when they made love, their bodies fulfilling the passion they had felt for so long . . .

'OK,' Ry groaned at last, releasing her. 'I can't bear much more of this without bursting a blood-vessel. You might as well tell me who that was on the telephone.'

'The hospital,' she replied, tracing the shape of his mouth with her fingers. 'They've got the results of Big Eddie's X-ray.'

'And?' he prompted.

'And there's no fracture. They're discharging him tomorrow.'

'Pity,' Ry said unfeelingly. 'I was convinced I'd at least cracked the brute's skull.'

'Don't you dare talk like that,' Ginny reproved. 'If he hadn't just been concussed, it could have serious for you.

The police said so—even though there were those two men who saw him attack you.' She gave him the sternest look she could muster, given that she was melting inside with love and desire for him. 'You need looking after, Ryan Savage. I don't know how you've managed without me for so long.'

'I don't know either,' he said gently. 'But I'm never going to try and manage without you again, Ginny. Not even for a moment.' He pulled her down into his arms, and she laid her cheek against his lean, muscular torso, closing her eyes in bliss. She heard his deep voice go on, 'This weekend has been the happiest of my life.'

'Despite spending the days talking non-stop, and the nights in bed with a girl who won't let you make love to her?'

'I'm learning self-control.' His arms drew her tight. 'You've been a part of me for so long. And yet I'm always aware of loving you. Of loving you, and needing you. Over these past weeks, I've wondered just how I managed to stay away for so long.'

'You said you had your reasons,' she said reflectively, tracing the line of his ribs with her fingertips. 'And I believe you.'

'If you touch me like that,' he said in a strained voice, 'I can't answer for my self-control.'

'Sorry,' Ginny sputtered with laughter, and laid the errant hand on his chest. 'Isn't it funny how pleased everyone is?'

'You mean about us?'

'Yes. Especially my mother. I haven't heard her laugh like that, or look so happy, since my dad died. She's so absolutely delighted about me and you. And all my friends are too . . . Everyone seems to be.'

'Don't sound so surprised. There are people who don't share your opinion that I'm a completely lost cause,' Ry said wryly.

'You're not a lost cause any more,' she pointed out

with a grin. 'You've got me to look after you.'

'And you've got me to look after *you,*' he reminded her with a touch of irony. 'You sometimes get these off-beat ideas that have to be checked. Like agreeing to marry Miles Langton. Not one of your best efforts.'

'No.' She shuddered as a chill memory of Miles and Jessica Langton, and the life she would have had with them, crossed her thoughts. 'God, when I think of it . . .'

'Don't think of it,' he advised. 'Not yet, anyway. In a couple of months you can look back on it and laugh at the whole mad episode.'

'I'll never laugh at it,' she said quietly. 'How could I ever laugh at almost losing you for ever?'

'Oh, you wouldn't have lost me for ever,' Ry smiled. 'If all else failed, I had Contingency Plan Number Nine.'

'Yes? And what was Contingency Plan Number Nine?' she wanted to know.

'If I couldn't talk you out of it before your wedding day, I was going to kidnap you in the dead of night, drag you off to London, and keep you locked in my coal-cellar until you saw reason.'

Ginny started to laugh, then stopped, seeing his eyes. 'You're serious!'

'Of course I'm serious,' he nodded. 'You mean much too much to me to ever let you marry another man. Let alone a man like Miles Langton.'

'And yet I thought he was so decent, so honourable . . .' she sighed.

'I didn't,' Ry retorted grimly. 'I knew him of old. When I was just a kid, my foster-father got involved with Miles Langton over a land deal. Miles made him an offer that was plainly illegal, that would have resulted in someone else losing a lot of money which they were entitled to. My foster-dad turned him down. He would have told the police, except that Miles had arranged things so that nothing could ever be traced back to him. He's been crooked for a long time, Ginny, and he knows

I know. That's why he's always been a bit shy of me.'

'Why didn't you tell me all this?' she asked, sighing again.

'Would you have believed me?' he challenged her drily. 'You seemed to have this built-in resistance to everything I tried to say about Miles Langton. Besides, the question at point was Miles's eligibility as a husband, not his honesty as a banker.'

'Miles just isn't eligible as a husband,' she said flatly. 'Jessica was right—the man is fundamentally unsuited to marriage. Oh, Ry,' she apologised miserably, 'I was crazy!' She closed her eyes, shuddering again. 'That's the only way I can put it. Crazy. Of course, I'd never have gone crazy in the first place if you hadn't left me alone for so long! What do you think will happen to him now, Ry? He ought to be made to pay. Why didn't you want us to tell the police about Miles paying Big Eddie to hurt you? That's a very serious offence. And I'll never forgive him for it.'

'Do you fancy the idea of spending the next few weeks in police stations and courtrooms, giving evidence, facing cross-examination? Going through a sordid trial, which would probably end up with that poor dumb ox Eddie going to prison, and Miles getting off with a fine he could easily pay?' Ry shook his head. 'I've been through the mill of prosecuting someone, Ginny.'

'Who?'

'Someone who tried to do me down in business. And I can assure you, there's no satisfaction at the end of it.'

'But there would be justice!' she said quickly.

'Let Margaret Easy decide on that. He's as much in her power now as she once was in his. After all, if she breathes a word of what he's done, he'll be ruined for ever. And she has suffered far worse at Miles's hands than either of us have. All I've got is a few bruises and a cut cheek.' Ry hugged her tight. 'And that's a very, very small price to pay for getting you back, cleanly and completely.'

'I wonder what she'll do to him,' Ginny sighed, snuggling into his embrace.

'That depends on how angry she is,' Ry shrugged.

'If it were up to me, I would force him to resign.'

'So would I. But judging by circumstances, she may have other ideas.' He smiled rather grimly. 'I have the strangest feeling, for example, that an unknown benefactor is going to clear off all Margaret's debts first thing this morning.'

Ginny thought of Margaret's beaming face last night, as she'd toasted them, and nodded. 'I got that impression too. Miles offered *me* ten thousand to keep quiet, so I expect he'll have offered Margaret a lot more.'

'I rather doubt, after the weekend Miles must have spent, whether he'll ever try anything crooked again.'

'Thank God I don't have to go back to the bank,' she mused. 'But I'm going to look for a job in another bank, Ry, as soon as we're married. I'm an experienced teller now, you know. It shouldn't be too hard to find a job in London. And then we'll be able to afford a decent place to live, and——'

'I don't want you working in any bank,' Ry interrupted gently. 'I want you to concentrate on your painting. That's where your future lies, I'm convinced of that. You might even take that art course . . . you have so much talent, my love. Putting you behind a till was a rotten idea, like most of Miles's ideas.'

'He was a rotten man. Mum knew he was rotten too. I never suspected she disliked him strongly until Saturday. She was hiding it all this time, because she thought it was what I wanted, and she didn't want to throw any shadows on my happiness. But she really hated the idea of my marrying him. I'm amazed she kept it in so well.'

'Mothers only want what's best for their daughters,' Ry smiled. 'You'll find that out yourself one day.'

'One day soon,' said Ginny. She propped herself up

on one elbow, and looked at him with dreamily smiling brown eyes. 'I want your babies, Ry. That's why I want to do my share of working—so we can afford the family I want. Painting's all very well, but it won't bring in much money over the next couple of years.'

'And how will all these babies you're planning fit on the back of my motorbike?' he asked, arching one eyebrow.

'You'll have to brace yourself and get a car,' she informed him. 'It's as simple as that.'

He laughed softly. 'A car? That shouldn't be too hard. I've got a hundred and ten to choose from.'

'Have you?' she smiled, not quite getting the joke.

'Mmm,' he nodded, sitting up and pulling her close. He cupped her face in his hands, and kissed her mouth firmly. 'I want you to promise you won't be angry with me, my love.'

'When?' asked Ginny, pleased by the kiss, but still perplexed.

'Later today. When we get to London, and I show you round the house. And . . . the business.'

'What business?' she demanded, frowning.

'My business.' Ry's eyes were dancing. 'Fortune Car Hire. Everything from a Range Rover to a Ferrari.'

She searched his face. 'Is that . . . is that who you work for?'

'They work for me. I own the firm, Ginny.' And as she stared at him blankly, Ry laughed, and kissed her parted lips. 'You do have some blind spots, Ginny darling. Did you really imagine I would ask you to marry me without the means to provide for you, and the brood of children you've obviously set your heart on?'

'I—I don't understand,' she stammered.

He grinned. 'No, of course you don't. You thought I was the kind of man who would give you a life on the back of a motorbike, wandering from pillar to post.' He quoted with wicked accuracy, 'An existence of dishonesty and laziness, wasn't it? Asking you to waste the rest of your life with me?'

'Oh, Ry!' Her face was crimson with humiliation. 'I can't believe I really talked like that. I don't know who I imagined I was.' She covered her face with her hands for a moment, then looked up at him, her curiosity overcoming her embarrassment at hearing her own crass words repeated. 'But are you serious? You own a business? *You*?'

'Yes, *me,*' he mimicked her tone. 'Don't you believe I'm capable of it yet?'

'Of course I do,' she said simply. 'I believe you're capable of anything in the world, if you set your heart on it.' She bit her lower lip hard. 'But Miles told me . . .'

Ry arched one eyebrow. '*Miles* told you?' The slight emphasis he put on the word 'Miles' made her gasp with sudden understanding.

'My God! Why was I such a simpleton as to believe him?' She wriggled upright, almost spitting with indignation. 'He told me you were some kind of a—a petty criminal. That you didn't have a job, or any money, and that you lived the most aimless, dissolute kind of life . . . He claimed he'd checked with your branch, and he had all sorts of statements and accounts to prove it!'

Ry smiled slightly. 'That sounds rather as though he actually did check with my branch. Because if he did, he would have realised that what he probably saw as his trump card—being richer than me—wasn't worth a damn any more.'

'Ry,' Ginny said in a small voice, 'please don't tell me you're *rich*. I couldn't bear it.'

'Depends what you call rich,' he said with an impious grin. 'I got this tan a long way from Lacon's farm, put it that way.'

'The Costa del Sol, I suppose,' she said, staring at him.

'Barbados, actually.'

'You've been going to places like Barbados without me?' she hissed. 'If you didn't have that bandage on your cheek——Just how wealthy are you?'

He kissed her, his expression amused. 'I haven't counted lately. I'm a long way off being a millionaire, Ginny. I've only been in business five years. But I do have three garages full of very smart luxury cars, and no shortage of customers to hire them. At highly competitive rates, of course. And every year, the business just goes up and up. Remember that Ferrari?'

'Yes,' Ginny whispered.

'It wasn't Keith Lacon's, it was one of my own. I just couldn't resist taking you out in it. I was going to show you everything that day, but you wouldn't come.' His voice gentled. 'I'm glad you didn't, now. Because now I know you'd have married me even if I hadn't had a bean in the world. You won't need to work in any bank, my love.' He touched her cheek. 'Though the offer means more to me than you can imagine. And as for a house, a few weeks ago I bought rather a nice place, on the edge of Hampstead Heath, with you in mind . . .'

She sat in silence, just staring at him, trying to take it in. Just remembering all the things she'd said to him over these past weeks. And wishing she'd bitten her tongue off first.

At last she said quietly, 'I think I can imagine why you didn't tell me before, Ry. And—and I've never felt so awful in my life.'

'Don't,' he chided, kissing her trembling mouth. 'And don't you dare start crying. I didn't really believe you'd changed utterly, and were now hooked on wealth. I just wanted to be sure you wanted me for my sake. It was also,' he added with a smile, 'rather fun pretending to be penniless Ry Savage again. The leafy lanes of our youth, and all that. God, I've missed you . . .' He gathered her in his arms, and for a long while they just lay there, the bright morning sun starting to peep through the curtains, splashing the bed with gold.

'That's what I was doing all those years,' Ry said,

after a long while. 'Waiting for you to grow up, and making enough money to give you all the things I dreamed of giving you. It started with a legacy from my father, when I was twenty-one. My real father, I mean.' Ry nodded as she looked up at him in surprise. 'Yes, I was just as taken aback. I'd hardly bothered thinking about my real parents since I was a kid. He's dead now, but it turned out he'd invested some money for me before he died, and it was quite a tidy sum by the time I came of age. I could have asked you to marry me then, but you were still in your teens—and I knew I had to have more than just an inheritance. I used the money to buy a broken-down car-hire business in West London, and . . .' He paused, looking down at her. 'But there's time enough to go into all that when we get to London.'

Ginny touched his long black hair almost timidly, and smiled. 'You have to admit that you don't exactly look like a business tycoon. Especially with that earring . . . and the bike . . . it's all rather shocking to Grantley's sensibilities, you know!'

'We'll be leaving Grantley a long way behind us,' he reminded her gently. 'We'll always be back for visits. But from now on, my love, our life is going to be in London. And you're going to love it.'

'I know I am.'

Ry kissed her hand. 'I told you,' he went on, 'I'll never go in for drab suits and conformity. Why should I, when that isn't me? My customers don't seem to mind.'

'Especially not the female ones, I expect,' she said tartly.

'I told you I'd reformed too. I mean it. I've changed a great deal inside, though I've never bothered to change my outward appearance. However, if you want me to,' he smiled, 'I'll get the hair shortened, and shed the earring.'

'Don't you *dare* cut your hair! It's so beautiful.' Ginny mused. 'But I've never liked that earring, ever since you told me it came from an admirer. And yet it suits you so perfectly. I'll have to buy you one of my own.'

'Then you'll take me as I am?'

'Yes. If you'll take *me* as I am.' She looked down. 'I've said and done some things I'll be ashamed of for the rest of my life,' she said in a low voice. 'I'm selfish and spoiled and badly behaved. But I'll try and reform too, Ry. God knows I need it. And I swear I'll make you a good wife!'

'I know you will.' He studied her face, reading the expression of almost childlike emotion on it. 'Well, well! I never expected to see the acid-tongued Ginny Northcliffe quite bowled over!'

'I feel as though I've just been dropped on my head out of an aeroplane,' she confessed. 'I feel as weak as a kitten . . .'

'Do you now?' Ry's eyes narrowed smokily. 'A bad man might seize an opportunity like this for his own wicked ends . . .'

'You wouldn't,' she protested weakly, as he unfastened the ribbon of her nightgown.

'I would,' he assured her, his mouth covering hers ruthlessly.

'You are all I've ever dreamed of,' she whispered, a little while later. She was feeling very small suddenly. Very small, very young, and yet very happy. 'I love you, Ry. I've always loved you, and I always will. But I almost wish—I almost wish you weren't rich.'

He laughed huskily. 'You'll get used to it.'

'But you were so lovely as a wild, romantic, irresponsible troublemaker . . .'

'I'll be just as lovely as a wild, romantic, utterly responsible husband,' he smiled. 'Just you wait and see.'

Ginny shook her head slowly. 'No, I can't wait any longer.' She watched his eyes react, and felt the desire begin to flood her own veins, like liquid gold. She reached up to slip her arms round his neck and whispered, 'I've changed my mind, my love. You and I have both been waiting for far too long already. Show me now. Show me *everything* . . .'

INDULGE A LITTLE SWEEPSTAKES

OFFICIAL RULES

SWEEPSTAKES RULES AND REGULATIONS. NO PURCHASE NECESSARY.

1. NO PURCHASE NECESSARY. To enter complete the official entry form and return with the invoice in the envelope provided. Or you may enter by printing your name, complete address and your daytime phone number on a 3 x 5 piece of paper. Include with your entry the hand printed words "Indulge A Little Sweepstakes." Mail your entry to: Indulge A Little Sweepstakes, P.O. Box 1397, Buffalo, NY 14269-1397. No mechanically reproduced entries accepted. Not responsible for late, lost, misdirected mail, or printing errors.

2. Three winners, one per month (Sept. 30, 1989, October 31, 1989 and November 30, 1989), will be selected in random drawings. All entries received prior to the drawing date will be eligible for that month's prize. This sweepstakes is under the supervision of MARDEN-KANE, INC. an independent judging organization whose decisions are final and binding. Winners will be notified by telephone and may be required to execute an affidavit of eligibility and release which must be returned within 14 days, or an alternate winner will be selected.

3. Prizes: 1st Grand Prize (1) a trip for two to Disneyworld in Orlando, Florida. Trip includes round trip air transportation, hotel accommodations for seven days and six nights, plus up to $700 expense money (ARV $3,500). 2nd Grand Prize (1) a seven-night Chandris Caribbean Cruise for two includes transportation from nearest major airport, accommodations, meals plus up to $1,000 in expense money (ARV $4,300). 3rd Grand Prize (1) a ten-day Hawaiian holiday for two includes round trip air transportation for two, hotel accommodations, sightseeing, plus up to $1,200 in spending money (ARV $7,700). All trips subject to availability and must be taken as outlined on the entry form.

4. Sweepstakes open to residents of the U.S. and Canada 18 years or older except employees and the families of Torstar Corp., its affiliates, subsidiaries and Marden-Kane, Inc. and all other agencies and persons connected with conducting this sweepstakes. All Federal, State and local laws and regulations apply. Void wherever prohibited or restricted by law. Taxes, if any are the sole responsibility of the prize winners. Canadian winners will be required to answer a skill testing question. Winners consent to the use of their name, photograph and/or likeness for publicity purposes without additional compensation.

5. For a list of prize winners, send a stamped, self-addressed envelope to Indulge A Little Sweepstakes Winners, P.O. Box 701, Sayreville, NJ 08871.

DL-SWPS

INDULGE A LITTLE SWEEPSTAKES

OFFICIAL RULES

SWEEPSTAKES RULES AND REGULATIONS. NO PURCHASE NECESSARY.

1. NO PURCHASE NECESSARY. To enter complete the official entry form and return with the invoice in the envelope provided. Or you may enter by printing your name, complete address and your daytime phone number on a 3 x 5 piece of paper. Include with your entry the hand printed words "Indulge A Little Sweepstakes." Mail your entry to: Indulge A Little Sweepstakes, P.O. Box 1397, Buffalo, NY 14269-1397. No mechanically reproduced entries accepted. Not responsible for late, lost, misdirected mail, or printing errors.

2. Three winners, one per month (Sept. 30, 1989, October 31, 1989 and November 30, 1989), will be selected in random drawings. All entries received prior to the drawing date will be eligible for that month's prize. This sweepstakes is under the supervision of MARDEN-KANE, INC. an independent judging organization whose decisions are final and binding. Winners will be notified by telephone and may be required to execute an affidavit of eligibility and release which must be returned within 14 days, or an alternate winner will be selected.

3. Prizes: 1st Grand Prize (1) a trip for two to Disneyworld in Orlando, Florida. Trip includes round trip air transportation, hotel accommodations for seven days and six nights, plus up to $700 expense money (ARV $3,500). 2nd Grand Prize (1) a seven-night Chandris Caribbean Cruise for two includes transportation from nearest major airport, accommodations, meals plus up to $1,000 in expense money (ARV $4,300). 3rd Grand Prize (1) a ten-day Hawaiian holiday for two includes round trip air transportation for two, hotel accommodations, sightseeing, plus up to $1,200 in spending money (ARV $7,700). All trips subject to availability and must be taken as outlined on the entry form.

4. Sweepstakes open to residents of the U.S. and Canada 18 years or older except employees and the families of Torstar Corp., its affiliates, subsidiaries and Marden-Kane, Inc. and all other agencies and persons connected with conducting this sweepstakes. All Federal, State and local laws and regulations apply. Void wherever prohibited or restricted by law. Taxes, if any are the sole responsibility of the prize winners. Canadian winners will be required to answer a skill testing question. Winners consent to the use of their name, photograph and/or likeness for publicity purposes without additional compensation

5. For a list of prize winners, send a stamped, self-addressed envelope to Indulge A Little Sweepstakes Winners, P.O. Box 701, Sayreville, NJ 08871.

© 1989 HARLEQUIN ENTERPRISES LTD.

DL-SWPS

INDULGE A LITTLE—WIN A LOT!

Summer of '89 Subscribers-Only Sweepstakes

OFFICIAL ENTRY FORM

This entry must be received by: October 31, 1989
This month's winner will be notified by: Nov. 7, 1989
Trip must be taken between: Dec. 7, 1989–April 7, 1990
(depending on sailing schedule)

YES, I want to win the Caribbean cruise vacation for two! I understand the prize includes round-trip airfare, a one-week cruise including private cabin and all meals, and a daily allowance as revealed on the "Wallet" scratch-off card.

Name ____________________

Address ____________________

City __________ State/Prov. ______ Zip/Postal Code ______

Daytime phone number ____________________
Area code

Return entries with invoice in envelope provided. Each book in this shipment has two entry coupons — and the more coupons you enter, the better your chances of winning!

DINDL-2

INDULGE A LITTLE—WIN A LOT!

Summer of '89 Subscribers-Only Sweepstakes

OFFICIAL ENTRY FORM

This entry must be received by: October 31, 1989
This month's winner will be notified by: Nov. 7, 1989
Trip must be taken between: Dec. 7, 1989–April 7, 1990
(depending on sailing schedule)

YES, I want to win the Caribbean cruise vacation for two! I understand the prize includes round-trip airfare, a one-week cruise including private cabin and all meals, and a daily allowance as revealed on the "Wallet" scratch-off card.

Name ____________________

Address ____________________

City __________ State/Prov. ______ Zip/Postal Code ______

Daytime phone number ____________________
Area code

Return entries with invoice in envelope provided. Each book in this shipment has two entry coupons — and the more coupons you enter, the better your chances of winning!

© 1989 HARLEQUIN ENTERPRISES LTD.

DINDL-2